WILDCATS

SLAM DUNK

BY JAKE MADDOX

ILLUSTRATED BY SEAN TIFFANY

Published by Stone Arch Books
A Capstone Imprint
151 Good Counsel Drive, P.O. Box 669
Mankato, Minnesota 56002
www.capstonepub.com

Printed in the United States of America in Stevens Point, Wisconsin.
032010
005741WZF10

First published in 2010 by Stone Arch Books as:

Playing Forward

On Guard

Win or Lose

Off the Bench

Library of Congress Cataloging-in-Publication Data
Maddox, Jake.
Wildcats slam dunk / written by Jake Maddox ; illustrated by Sean Tiffany.
p. cm. – (A Jake Maddox sports story)
ISBN 978-1-4342-2886-4 (pbk.)
[1. Basketball–Fiction. 2. Teamwork (Sports)–Fiction.] I. Tiffany, Sean, ill. II. Title.
PZ7.M25643Wil 2010
[Fic]–dc22
2010007400

Summary: Four stories about the Wildcats Basketball team.
Photo Credits: ShutterStock/Mike Flippo (p. 208)

TABLE OF CONTENTS

26 ISAAC ROTH

WILDCATS

WILDCATS

		Position	PPG	FT %	FG		
	Danny Powell	Center	9	73.2	82.		22
11	Daniel Friedland	Forward	5.7	95.8	85.1	12	10
13	PJ Harris	Center	22	65.6	90.2	7	32
23	Trey Smith Ⓒ	Guard	14	96.2	80.5	20	8
26	Isaac Roth	Guard	11.5	94.1	79.3	11	6
33	Dwayne Illy	Forward	6.2	82.9	77.9	9	13

Highlight: **Isaac Roth**

TABLE OF CONTENTS

··· Chapter 1 ···

ALL-STAR

Isaac Roth and his father sat on the edge of their seats. It was the first game for Westfield High School's basketball team. Isaac's older brother Eli was their forward.

Isaac watched his brother on the court. He was tall — six feet and three inches. When Eli got the ball, everyone watching knew they were in for a show. Eli was a great ball-handler, and had a great outside shot. In fact, he almost never missed. But that's not why the fans cheered. Eli was at his best when he drove hard to the hoop.

It was already the fourth quarter. Westfield High was up by fifteen points, and everyone knew they'd win.

Still, when the point guard passed to Eli, the place went crazy.

"Eli, Eli!" the crowd chanted.

Isaac's brother faked a shot from the top of the key, then dribbled low past his defender, down the lane, and to the basket. He faked out the opposing center and leaped at the hoop. A hush fell over the crowd.

SLAM!

The crowd exploded with cheers as Eli's slam dunk hit home. Eli's size-thirteen sneakers hit the wood with a thud. He smiled as he pumped his fist. Isaac and his dad jumped to their feet and cheered with everyone else.

"Hey, Dad," Isaac said over the roar of the crowd. "Look at that!" He pointed across the court at a small group of girls.

His dad squinted across the court. "Those girls?" he said. "What about them?"

"Wait a second," Isaac said.

A moment later, as the girls jumped and cheered, they turned around and faced the crowd, screaming and shouting.

Then Dad saw the backs of their shirts. Each shirt had one word across the top of their backs, just like Eli's jersey: "ROTH."

Dad laughed. "Well, now I've seen everything," he said. "My son has his own cheerleaders."

Isaac laughed too. He didn't want to admit that he was jealous.

He loved basketball too, and was even pretty good. But at only five feet and four inches tall, he couldn't make impressive shots and dunks like his brother could.

"Do you think I'll ever be as good as Eli?" he asked his dad.

"You're a great basketball player, Isaac," Dad replied.

"Thanks," Isaac said. "But I'm so short, especially compared to Eli. I'll never be able to do the things he does."

Dad put an arm around his younger son's shoulders. "You're only thirteen, Isaac," Dad said gently. "You'll get taller. After all, Eli wasn't always as tall as he is now."

Isaac didn't say anything, but he thought, *Yeah, but he was always way taller than me.*

Before long, the game was over. Eli had scored a total of 34 points, more than any other player. Total strangers were clapping him on the back and giving him high fives as he left the court. Isaac even saw the girls in the "ROTH" jerseys run over and give him hugs and kiss his cheek.

"Are we going to wait for Eli to get changed?" Isaac asked his dad.

"Of course," Dad said. "But let's wait outside where it's cool. It's hot in that gym."

The two of them leaned against their car to wait for Eli.

The sun was down, and the night was a cool relief after the stuffy gymnasium.

"Tryouts are next week for the middle school team," Isaac said.

"Are you excited?" Dad asked.

Isaac shrugged. "Yeah, I guess," he said. "But I'm nervous, too."

"Ah, you'll make the team, no sweat," Dad said.

"But I want to start," Isaac said. "I want to be the starting power forward, like Eli."

"Well," Dad said, "I'm sure you'll make the starting five. Any position would be great, right?"

Isaac didn't say anything. Just then, Eli pushed through the heavy metal double doors on the side of the gym.

"Hey!" Eli called as he walked up.

"Great game, all-star," Dad said.

"Thanks, Dad," Eli said.

The three of them climbed into the car. Eli sat in the front, and Isaac got into the back seat.

"Isaac was just saying tryouts for the middle school team are next week," Dad said as they drove toward home.

"Oh yeah?" Eli said, looking back at Isaac. "Is Coach Turnbull still the man down there?"

"Yup," Isaac said, leaning forward. "He coached me last year, too. I didn't start last year, though. This year I hope I will."

"Oh, no doubt," Eli said. "You'll definitely make the starting five with your speed. I bet he'll make you point guard."

Isaac sighed. "I want to play power forward," he said. "That's where the points are. That's who everyone cheers for!"

Eli shrugged. "You've got the skills for point guard, little brother," he said. "Little guy, lots of speed, and you're sharp, too."

"'Little' is right," Isaac said under his breath.

"Besides," Eli added, "do you think no one ever cheered for Chris Paul, or Steve Nash, or John Stockton? Or Magic Johnson?"

Isaac sat back and slouched in the dark of the back seat. He leaned against the window and looked out at the white streetlights over the road as they whizzed past them.

I don't care about those guys. I want to play power forward, Isaac thought. *Like my big brother.*

··· Chapter 2 ···
TRYOUTS

The tryouts were held the next Monday, right after the last class of the day. Isaac got changed into his shorts and last year's jersey in the locker room. Then he jogged out to the court.

"Hey, Isaac," PJ Harris said. PJ was the tallest member of the team. In fact, he was the tallest student at Westfield Middle School. If one player had the height to go pro one day, it was PJ.

"Ready for tryouts?" PJ asked. He held out his hand for a high five.

Isaac slapped his friend's hand. "Of course," he said. "I'm pretty sure I'll be starting this season. You will too. No doubt."

"Of course," PJ said. The two boys turned as the locker room door swung open and Dwayne Illy strode in.

"There's my competition," Isaac said.

"Are you hoping for power forward this season?" PJ asked. "Huh."

"What do you mean, 'huh'?" Isaac said.

PJ put his hands up and smiled. "Nothing, nothing," he said. "Dwayne is just really good at getting to the hoop. He's amazing from the foul line, too."

"I have a great free throw," Isaac said. "You know that. Better than yours!"

PJ laughed. "Man, my grandma's free throw is better than mine," he said.

Suddenly a whistle blew. PJ and Isaac turned and saw Coach Turnbull at the center of the court. All of the guys who were trying out gathered around him in a circle.

"All right, welcome to tryouts," Coach Turnbull said. "We're going to run drills and play a few short scrimmage games so I can get a good idea of what everyone can do out there."

Isaac glanced at Dwayne Illy. Dwayne was smiling.

He's so confident, Isaac thought. He wished he felt as sure of himself as Dwayne did.

Coach T opened a big equipment bag at his feet and pulled out a bunch of red and yellow scrimmage jerseys. Each jersey was numbered.

"I'm going to call out numbers while you play," the coach said. "If I call your number, call back with your name so I know who you are. If you were on the team last year, I already know who you are, and you can wear your jersey from last year."

Each of the players grabbed a jersey. Isaac and PJ both grabbed red jerseys. Dwayne picked up a yellow one.

Before the scrimmage, Coach Turnbull wanted the players to start with a layup drill.

"Perfect," Isaac said to PJ as they lined up. "Dwayne's on the other team. This way I can show him up during the scrimmage. Steal off him, block his shots — really give him a hard time."

PJ shook his head. "You're fast, Isaac," he said. "And you know all of Coach T's plays better than anyone."

"What's your point?" Isaac asked.

It was his turn to take a layup. He jogged up, caught his pass, and laid up the basketball. It went in off the backboard.

PJ jogged up next. "What I'm trying to say," he said as he shot his own layup, "is that you're a born point guard."

"Yeah, everyone keeps saying that," Isaac said. "But that's the problem. I don't want to play point guard."

After drills, Coach T called everyone to the middle to start the first scrimmage. Isaac and PJ were on a team with Trey Smith, a great shooter they both knew.

"Hey, Trey," Isaac said, calling him over.

Trey jogged over to PJ and Isaac. "What's up?" he said.

"You take the ball up, okay?" Isaac said.

Trey looked surprised. "Me?" he said. "You want me to play point?"

Isaac nodded, and Trey shrugged. "All right, I'll give it a shot," he said.

Isaac gave him a high five and the coach blew his whistle to start the scrimmage.

"No jump, Coach T?" PJ asked.

"Let's just say red ball to start," the coach said, smiling. "I think we all know PJ Harris would win a jump against anyone else in this gym."

Isaac threw in to Trey to start play. Then Isaac moved quickly down the court. He called out to Trey, "I'm open!"

Trey launched a pass to him, and Isaac barely got it. It was far off to the left. Isaac was able to spin through the yellow team's defense. He shot a quick layup.

"Yes!" he said as the ball fell in for two points.

"Nice recovery, Isaac," Coach T called out.

On defense, Isaac stayed close to Dwayne Illy. When a pass came to Dwayne on the yellow team's first play, Isaac managed to knock it out of bounds.

Dwayne glared at him. "What?" Isaac said, but Dwayne just turned away.

The next time up the court, Trey had trouble finding an open man. Isaac finally came to the top of the key and behind Trey.

"Give it here," Isaac said. Trey tossed him the ball, then moved toward the hoop. Isaac passed him the ball on one bounce. Trey shot and scored.

"Nice shot, Trey," the coach said. "And nice assist, Isaac. Way to take charge out there."

This time on defense, Isaac was playing Dwayne even tighter. Dwayne caught a pass and tried to fake out Isaac, but Isaac wasn't fooled. He tapped the ball out of Dwayne's hands and grabbed it. Then Isaac took off on a fast break.

"Great steal, Isaac!" PJ shouted, clapping.

Isaac reached the hoop and laid it up easily. Two more points.

The whistle blew. "Isaac, take a seat," the coach said. "Let's see how they do without you."

Isaac sat down on the bench. *This is a cinch,* he thought. *I'll definitely be the starting power forward.*

··· Chapter 3 ···

THE LINEUP

"Hey, Isaac," PJ said. He stuck his head into the cafeteria and waved at Isaac. "You coming to Coach T's office? The starting lineup is posted."

Isaac popped a last tater tot into his mouth and nodded. "On my way," he said with his mouth full. After he dropped his empty tray at the return counter, he jogged after PJ.

"The list has been up for at least ten minutes by now," PJ said. "We'll be the last two to check it, I bet."

Isaac shrugged as he jogged beside PJ toward Coach Turnbull's office. "I'm not worried," he said. "I already know what the list is going to say. Isaac Roth, starting power forward."

Just then, Dwayne Illy passed them, going the other direction. He looked at Isaac and smiled. "No hard feelings, Isaac," Dwayne said, and jogged on.

"What was that all about?" PJ asked.

"He was just being a good loser, I guess," Isaac said, "since he didn't get starting power forward. After tryouts on Monday there's no way the coach chose someone else over me."

PJ and Isaac rounded the corner. Then they stopped in front of the office door that read "Athletics Department." The team lineup was posted on the corkboard.

PJ leaned down to look at the list. "Uh-oh," he said.

"What?" Isaac asked, pushing PJ out of the way. "Didn't you make the team?"

"Sure," PJ said. "Starting center."

"So why the uh-oh?" Isaac asked. Then he saw it. "Starting power forward, Dwayne Illy," he said slowly.

Isaac looked at PJ. PJ nodded. "I guess you're our new point guard," PJ said.

Isaac curled his hands into fists. "I can't believe this!" he said. "What was Coach T thinking?" Then he pounded on the office door.

"Come in," the coach called. Isaac pushed the door open.

"Coach T, how could you make Dwayne power forward?" Isaac asked. "I played way better than he did yesterday."

"Yes, you did," the coach said. "But you'll do more for the team at point guard."

"More for the team?" Isaac said. "Point guards hardly ever score!"

"No, they assist," the coach said.

"But what about all my steals," Isaac said, "and doing better than Dwayne so many times at tryouts?"

"Dwayne is a great power forward," Coach T said. "You're a great point guard, and that's final."

"I don't want to play point guard," Isaac said.

"Well, you don't have to be on the team, of course," the coach said. He got up to lead Isaac out of his office.

"That's it, huh?" Isaac asked angrily.

The coach nodded. "If you want to be in the starting five, you're our point guard," he said.

Isaac stepped into the hall. Coach T closed the door behind him.

"Where's Dwayne?" Isaac asked.

PJ looked at him. "Um, eating lunch, I think," he said. "Why?"

Isaac took off like a shot. He was a fast runner. Seconds later, he was heading into the cafeteria.

He found Dwayne sitting at a big table by the window. Isaac stepped right up to him.

"Dwayne, you know you don't deserve to have power forward instead of me," Isaac said.

Dwayne just looked at him and frowned.

Isaac lightly pushed Dwayne's shoulder. "Well?" Isaac said. "Aren't you going to say anything?"

Dwayne just shook his head and went back to eating his hamburger.

Isaac grunted in frustration. Then he turned and headed for the door.

··· Chapter 4 ···
FIRST PRACTICE

The team's first practice was that afternoon. Isaac didn't want to go.

"What's the point?" he asked PJ as they walked toward the locker room. "Coach T said I shouldn't bother coming if I won't play point guard."

"Right, but he meant that he wants you to show up," PJ said. "He wants you to play point guard."

"Yeah, I know," Isaac said, sighing.

The two boys got changed for practice and headed into the gym. Most of the team was already shooting around. After a few minutes, Coach Turnbull blew his whistle.

"Let's just start easy for our first practice, guys," the coach said. "Everybody, line up for layup drills."

He blew his whistle again. All of the players got into two lines for layups.

When it was Isaac's turn, he slowly jogged to the basket and tossed the ball up. It went in, but barely.

The coach said, "I know I said we'd take it easy, but show a little hustle out there, okay, Isaac?"

Isaac laughed. "It went in, didn't it?" he said. Then he went to the back of the rebound line.

"Watch the bad attitude, Isaac," the coach replied, frowning.

After drills, the boys split up into red and yellow teams for a scrimmage, just like they had during tryouts.

Isaac and Dwayne Illy ended up on the red team together.

"Great," Isaac said sarcastically. "This will be really fun. I have to play on a team with the guy who stole my position."

PJ won the tip-off for the yellow team, and they scored two points right away. The red team brought the ball up the court. Isaac dribbled at the top of the key, looking for an open man to pass to.

Dwayne cut across the key and Isaac tossed him the ball. But it flew past Dwayne, landing a couple of steps behind him.

"Yellow ball," the coach said as the ball went out of bounds.

"Oh, well," Isaac said with a shrug.

Dwayne glared at him.

"What?" Isaac asked. Dwayne just shook his head.

The next time Isaac was at the top of the key, the yellow team was up 4-0.

Dwayne got open again, and Isaac passed him the basketball. It flew at Dwayne like a bullet, this time a few steps ahead of him. Dwayne couldn't get to the pass in time.

PJ caught the pass instead. He threw it up the court at Trey Smith for the fast break. Now it was 6-0.

"You're going to lose the game for us," Dwayne said quietly to Isaac. "Unless you start playing like you care."

"Me?" Isaac shouted back. Everyone turned around. "Both of those failed drives were your fault!"

The coach jogged over and got between the boys. "What's the problem here?" Coach Turnbull asked.

"Dwayne is," Isaac said. "He missed both of my perfect passes, and he's blaming me because we're losing."

"Perfect passes?" Dwayne said. "Man, you must be crazy."

"Dwayne," the coach said, "go and have a seat on the bench for a minute."

"Me?" Dwayne said, looking surprised. "What did I do?"

"Just go, Dwayne," Coach Turnbull said. Dwayne sighed. Then he walked toward the bench.

"Isaac," the coach said, looking at him. "You played better in tryouts."

"Are you kidding? You're blaming me?" Isaac snapped. "First Dwayne was moving too fast and my pass went behind him. Then he was going way too slow, so my pass went in front of him. That guy can't play!"

"This isn't about blame," the coach replied. "This is about you. You haven't made an effort since we started drills an hour ago. Don't let your feelings about playing point guard affect your game, or you won't be on the team for long. Is that clear?"

"Oh, come on, Coach," Isaac said.

"Is it clear?" the coach asked again.

Isaac nodded. Coach Turnbull walked away and blew his whistle, then shouted to everyone, "Let's play ball."

··· Chapter 5 ···

FIRST GAME

The first game of the season was at the end of the week. PJ and Isaac sat on the bench in the Wildcats locker room, tying up their sneakers.

"Are you still mad?" PJ asked.

Isaac sighed. "To be honest," he said, "yes."

"You need to get over it before Coach T kicks you off the team for good," PJ said. He stood up and bounced on his toes.

"I can shoot and dribble circles around Dwayne," Isaac said. "And you know it."

PJ shook his head. "Whatever. Let's just play, okay?" he said.

The two boys headed out to the gym. The team gathered around the coach.

The starters stood, and everyone else sat on the team bench. Other students and parents sat in the bleachers. They cheered as the Westfield Middle School Wildcats took the court.

PJ won the tipoff for the Wildcats and got the ball to Isaac right away. Isaac brought the ball up to the key and called a play. Dwayne would have to get open.

Isaac dribbled well. He controlled the ball with his right hand, staying out of reach of his defender.

Dwayne didn't have much trouble getting open. Isaac spotted him and passed the ball.

Dwayne hurried, but he didn't get to the ball in time. It flew out of bounds off a defender's fingers.

"Still Westfield ball," the referee called out.

"Nice catch, Dwayne," Isaac said with a laugh, rolling his eyes.

"Oh, you think it's my fault?" Dwayne said angrily.

The coach called to Dwayne, "Keep your eyes open out there, Dwayne! That was a good pass."

Isaac smiled smugly at Dwayne, but he could see that Dwayne was mad.

After the throw in, Isaac took the ball to the top of the key and called the play again. He glanced up at the basket.

I should just get the two points myself, he thought. *Dwayne can't catch a pass anyway.*

Dwayne darted across the lane, and he got open for a few moments here and there. Isaac could have passed to him, but he didn't. Instead, he faked a jump shot, drove down the lane, and went for the layup.

But just as his foot left the ground, he got blocked by a defender who was nearly as tall as PJ. Isaac ended up on his butt in the paint.

"Time out!" Coach Turnbull called. He strode out to where Isaac sat on the court.

The coach leaned over and gave Isaac his hand to help him up. "Are you all right?" the coach asked as Isaac got up.

"Yeah," Isaac said with a nod.

"Good," the coach said. "I'm not happy," he added.

Isaac looked at the coach's face. It was beet red.

"If you pull another stunt like that," Coach Turnbull went on, "you're off the team. Dwayne was open five times, and you know it."

"What?" Isaac said, shocked.

"You heard me," the coach replied. He turned to the ref and nodded, then walked back to the Wildcats bench.

The referee blew his whistle. "Let's go," he said. "Visitor ball."

Isaac stomped his foot once, then fell back on defense. It was going to be a long game.

··· Chapter 6 ···

The next day, Isaac left lunch a few minutes early and headed down the hall toward the athletics department.

Coach Turnbull's office door stood open. Isaac stuck his head inside. "Hey, Coach," he said.

"Come on in, Isaac," the coach said. He put down the papers he'd been looking at. "What's happening?"

Isaac sat down across from Coach Turnbull. "I want to make a deal with you," he said.

"What kind of deal?" the coach asked.

"Let me try playing power forward," Isaac said.

"Isaac, we've been over this," the coach said.

"Let me finish," Isaac said. "I'm just talking about one practice. One scrimmage."

"That's it?" the coach asked.

Isaac nodded. "That's it," he said. "If I can show you I'm better than Dwayne Illy, you'll move me to that position permanently."

"I don't know," Coach Turnbull said.

"And," Isaac went on, "if I am really better at point guard, I'll drop the issue forever and play point guard like you want."

The coach narrowed his eyes and stared at Isaac. "Hmm," he said.

"Is it a deal?" Isaac asked.

The coach stood up and nodded, then put out his hand. "Deal," he said.

Isaac smiled and shook the coach's hand. "All right!" he said. "Thanks, Coach."

"Now get to class," Coach Turnbull said, sitting back down.

Finally, Isaac thought as he jogged to his next class. *I'll prove to everyone that I belong at power forward.*

··· Chapter 7 ···
SOMETHING NEW

"Listen up, everyone," Coach Turnbull said that afternoon in practice. "We're going to try some new positions today."

The other guys on the team whispered and looked around. Isaac snuck a glance at Dwayne, who was frowning.

PJ's eyebrows went up and he glanced at Isaac. "What is this?" he whispered, but Isaac just smiled.

"Dwayne Illy, I want you at point guard today," the coach said.

"Wait a second," Dwayne said. "What? I don't play point guard."

"And Isaac Roth will be playing power forward," Coach Turnbull went on. "They'll be leading the yellow team. Everyone else, grab a jersey and let's get a five-on-five scrimmage started."

No one said anything, but Isaac could tell that the other players were surprised.

The yellow team got the ball first. Dwayne dribbled well and stood at the top of the key to call a play. Then he called the first play.

Isaac knew all the plays perfectly, since he normally called them. The play that Dwayne called meant the power forward would fall back for a sneak pass, and then drive up for a layup.

Isaac headed back toward Dwayne, but just then Dwayne passed to PJ at the baseline. PJ managed to catch the pass and tried to lay it up, but he was under the backboard. The ball bounced off the bottom and rolled out of bounds.

The coach blew his whistle. "Wrong play, Dwayne," he said. "You called for Isaac to come back, but then you passed to PJ. No one was ready for it."

"Sorry, Coach," Dwayne said. "I'm not used to playing point guard."

"All right, play ball," the coach said. He tossed the ball in to the red team.

On the yellow team's next drive, Dwayne took his time at the top of the key. He called a play for Trey Smith, but when Trey got open, Dwayne didn't pass him the ball.

"Trey is open!" Isaac called out. "Dwayne, come on, figure it out!"

Dwayne struggled at the top of the key, and then passed to Isaac.

Isaac tried to drive. He managed to lose a defender, but two other red team players swarmed over him. One of them stole the ball and threw it down the court for an easy fast break.

"You called for Trey and didn't pass to him," Isaac told Dwayne. "He was wide open."

"I meant to call you up," Dwayne said. "Sorry. This is all new to me."

Isaac sighed. "It's cool," he said.

The next drive, Dwayne called the right play and passed to Isaac.

Isaac drove hard to the basket. He lost both defenders and put up a layup, but a strong arm fell over him and knocked him to the wood. The coach blew his whistle.

"Foul," Coach Turnbull said. "Take two, Isaac."

Isaac went to the line. He almost never took foul shots, but he had a good outside shot. He looked at the rim, raised the ball, and shot.

Swish!

"Nice one," the coach said.

On the next shot, the other players lining the lane got ready for the rebound.

Isaac shot, but this time the ball fell to the right. PJ got the rebound and laid it up for two more.

"Good one, PJ!" Dwayne said.

When the red team was winning 18-8, the yellow team brought the ball up again.

Dwayne called a play. Isaac had to cut across the lane, then go right back, losing his defender. Dwayne would pass to him right in the middle of the lane, and Isaac should have an easy layup.

But Dwayne had the play backward. When Isaac cut across, Dwayne threw a pass like a rocket.

Isaac was facing the wrong way. The ball hit Isaac right in the back of the head, and he fell to the floor like a sack of bricks.

··· Chapter 8 ···

BORN TO PLAY

Isaac got to his feet. He charged toward Dwayne. Someone yelled, "Fight!" But before Isaac could tackle Dwayne, Coach Turnbull pulled him away.

"No fighting!" the coach said.

"He beamed me in the head!" Isaac shouted, staring at Dwayne.

"It was an accident," Dwayne said. "I had the play backward. I'm used to seeing it from the other side, that's all."

"Oh, please," Isaac said. "You did it on purpose."

"It was an accident," the coach said.

"No way," Isaac said. He crossed his arms and looked at his sneakers. "He's blowing it, Coach."

The coach laughed. "He sure is," he said. "That's the point, Isaac. Dwayne isn't a general out there. He isn't usually keeping track of everyone's job and everyone's position."

Dwayne sat down on the bench and wiped his head with a towel. Isaac watched him catch his breath.

"You see, Isaac," the coach went on, "Dwayne's head is on his defender, and thinking about how to get another ball in that basket."

"So he's not a point guard," Isaac said.

"No, you are," Coach Turnbull said gently. "Your head is on everything at every moment. So yeah, you're small, and you can't weave through defenders as well as Dwayne. But you're doing something really important. You're leading the team on the court."

Isaac thought about it. It wasn't about being worse or better than Dwayne. It was about being right for point guard. "I get it, Coach," he said. Suddenly, instead of feeling small, he felt proud.

"All right then," the coach said. He turned to the bench. "Dwayne, come on in at power forward."

Dwayne smiled and jumped to his feet. He jogged out to the court.

"Play ball," the coach said. "Maybe we'll finally see some good plays today!"

The team laughed and the scrimmage began again. The yellow team brought the ball up. Isaac held it at the top of the key and called Dwayne across the lane. They connected perfectly.

Dwayne caught the pass and spun to his left, then back to his right. He easily shook his defender and went to the hoop.

Two points!

"Nice moves, Dwayne," Isaac said.

Dwayne laughed and said, "Nice pass, Isaac."

Isaac passed to Dwayne over and over. The two scored fourteen points for the yellow team.

Just before five o'clock, Isaac looked up and saw his father and brother sitting in the bleachers. They were a little early to pick him up from practice.

Isaac waved, and his brother waved back.

The red team took the ball up. Their forward drove to the hoop, but PJ stopped him with a perfect block. The ball rebounded right to Isaac.

Isaac spun and signaled to Dwayne to get down the court quickly. Right away, Dwayne took off like a shot, and Isaac passed the ball just ahead of him.

It was a perfect pass. Dwayne caught it and, after one dribble, easily laid it up for another two points.

"Great play, guys," the coach said. He blew his whistle. "That's it for today. I think we finally have a real point guard. Good job, Isaac."

Isaac smiled. He went over to his brother and father.

"When did you two get here?" Isaac asked.

"A while ago," his father said. "We missed your first game, so we wanted to see you in action."

Dwayne walked up. "This is Dwayne Illy," Isaac said. "He's our power forward."

"You two are some team," Isaac's dad said.

"Great assists, little brother," Eli said. "I didn't know you were so good. Point guard is a tough position."

"Nah," Isaac said. "Like you said, I have the right skills for it."

Isaac glanced at Dwayne. "Isn't that right, Dwayne?" he said.

"Oh, for sure," Dwayne replied.

"It would be ridiculous," Isaac added, "for me to play any other position."

"Yeah," Dwayne said. "It would be like if I played point guard."

"We better not ever let that happen," Isaac said. Dwayne and Isaac high-fived and laughed as they headed out to the parking lot.

ON GUARD

WILDCATS

Scoring/Shooting

#	Athlete Name	Position	PPG	FT %	FG %	Stl	Re
6	Danny Powell	Center	9	73.2	82.8	5	2:
11	Daniel Friedland	Forward	5.7	95.8	85.1	12	10
13	PJ Harris	Center	22	65.6	90.2	7	3:
23	Trey Smith Ⓒ	Guard	14	96.2	80.5	20	8
26	Isaac Roth	Guard	11.5	94.1	79.3	11	6
33	Dwayne Illy	Forward	6.2	82.9	77.9	9	13

Highlight: **Trey Smith**

TABLE OF CONTENTS

··· **Chapter 1** ···

SMITH SMITHEREENS

A banner hung across the gate at the entrance to Harding County Park, just outside of Westfield. The big sign read, "Smith Family Reunion."

Just past the gate, dozens of cars were parked in the lot. There were sedans, new and old; station wagons covered in bumper stickers; SUVs, some shiny, some covered in mud.

And just past the lot, near the picnic tables, cousins Trey and Pete Smith were leaning back on their bench. Each boy was holding a paper cup. They were taking a break from their basketball game.

"Ready?" eighth-grader Trey asked. He crushed his paper cup in his hand, then threw it into a nearby garbage can. "Two points."

Pete, who was in sixth grade, took a long drink from his own cup. "Ahh," he said. "Grandma's lemonade is so good." Then he jumped up, crushed his cup, and shot it toward the garbage can. It went in.

"I'm ready," Pete said. "Let's get out there."

Together, the two boys walked out of the shade and headed over to the basketball courts.

Most of the other Smith family boys, and several of the girls, were hanging around. Some were just watching, but others were taking some shots.

"Look out, everybody. We're back," Trey announced.

"So, any more challengers?" Pete added. "The Smith Smithereens are ready to play some more two-on-two."

Pete, though he wasn't the oldest cousin, was one of the best basketball players in the family. And when he teamed up with Trey — like he always did — no one could beat them.

"We'll take you two on," a voice said.

Trey and Pete turned around.

It was Uncle Rob and his daughter Jessa.

"Jessa and I have been practicing," Uncle Rob added.

Trey and Pete laughed and high-fived each other.

"No problem," Trey said. He called over to one of his cousins for the ball.

"Let's do it," Pete said.

Uncle Rob and Jessa started with the ball. Rob was much taller than both boys, and Jessa, who was fifteen, was as tall as Trey.

Still, when Rob took his first shot, Pete jumped up and knocked the ball right into Trey's hands.

"Ha!" Pete shouted. "That was a nice shot, Uncle Rob."

Trey drove the ball fast up the court and scored an easy two points.

Rob and Jessa looked at each other and rolled their eyes, but that didn't stop Trey and Pete. The cousins continued to shoot and score. After every basket, block, or steal, the two Smith boys would high-five and holler. They felt great, and they quickly had an unbeatable lead.

By the time the game was over, the score was 21 to 4. Trey's dad had shown up to watch the end. He stood on the sidelines next to Uncle Theo, Pete's dad.

"Well, there's no doubt about it," Uncle Rob said. He looked worn out. "You two are a great team."

"Thanks," Pete said, smiling.

"I wonder, though," Trey's father said. "What would happen if these two played against each other for once?"

"Might be interesting to see," Uncle Theo agreed.

"Pff," Trey said, waving them off. He threw an arm around his cousin's shoulder. "We'll never play against each other. Me and Pete, we're a team."

Pete nodded. "Right," he said. "Together, we'll beat anyone."

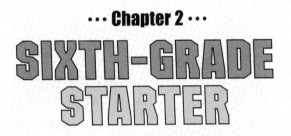

··· **Chapter 2** ···

SIXTH-GRADE STARTER

A few weeks later, the Westfield Middle School basketball team held tryouts. No one was surprised when Trey was named starting shooting guard and captain of the team.

The night of the tryouts, Trey went home and went straight to his family computer. He had to tell his cousin Pete the good news.

Hey, Pete, Trey typed in his instant message program.

What's up, cuz? Pete replied.

Guess who's going to be captain of the Westfield Middle School basketball team this season? Trey typed. *And starting shooting guard . . .*

Pete typed back, *Way to go, Trey! But guess what? I'm starting shooting guard for East Lake, and I'm only in sixth grade. HA!*

Trey couldn't believe it. He knew his cousin Pete was a great basketball player, but starting in sixth grade? That was really great. In fact, it was pretty much unheard of.

Trey hadn't been a starter until he was in seventh grade, and most players he knew didn't start until eighth grade, if they got to start at all.

Wow! Trey typed. *That's amazing, Pete.*

You know what this means, right? Pete typed. *Our dads are going to get their wish.*

What wish? Trey typed.

To see us play against each other for once, Pete replied.

Trey grabbed his backpack from the couch and pulled out the papers Coach Turnbull had given him. He quickly flipped through them until he found the one titled "Schedule."

He ran his finger down the page, but didn't have to look far. *Oh man!* he typed to his cousin. *The Wildcats play East Lake. Next week!*

··· Chapter 3 ···
IT'S ON!

Early that Saturday morning, Trey and Pete met at a local park. They often did, to challenge other guys to two-on-two games. Just like at the family reunion, they rarely lost.

Pete was on the court, shooting free throws, when Trey walked up. "Hey, cuz," Trey said.

Pete spun around. "Think fast," he said.

He passed the ball to Trey. It moved like a rocket, but Trey was quick. He caught the pass, and the ball made a loud slap as it hit his palms.

Trey smiled, then glanced at the hoop. He raised the ball, drew it back, and shot. Swish!

"For three!" Trey said. He jogged over to the basket and grabbed the ball.

Pete held up his hands for a pass. "Give it here," he said. "It's still too early for two-on-two, I guess."

"Yeah," Trey said. "No one else is around."

Trey passed the ball to Pete. "We can just shoot around until some other people show up," Trey said.

Pete took a shot from the baseline for two. "Swish!" he called as the ball fell. "I have a better idea than shooting around," he added. "Let's make this more interesting."

Trey grabbed the rebound and dribbled up to the foul line. "What do you mean?" he asked. Then he made a perfect free throw.

"Let's play some one-on-one," Pete said. He jogged to the basket and picked up the ball before it rolled onto the grass around the court. "It will be like a sneak preview for next week's game."

Trey narrowed his eyes at his cousin. "That could be fun," he said. "You can start, since I have the advantage in, let's see . . ." Trey counted off on his fingers, "Height, age, skill, good looks . . ."

"Ha ha," Pete replied. He dribbled up to the foul line. "You ready?"

Trey smiled and nodded. "Bring it, young fella," he said.

Pete faked a shot, but didn't fool Trey at all. Then Pete started to his left and went right.

That didn't fool Trey either. He knew Pete so well, he knew there was no way Pete was going left. Pete was always much faster moving to his right.

Trey stayed with him to the basket, but Pete managed to sink the layup.

"Good D, cuz," Pete said.

Trey grabbed the ball and took it to the line.

"Not good enough, though," Pete added with a smirk.

Trey grunted. "Just watch this," he said.

The two boys played one-on-one all morning. Even when some other guys showed up for two-on-two, Trey and Pete didn't stop their tournament.

They played game after game to 21 points, and neither of them ever won by much.

The boys decided to play one more game before lunch. Soon, the score was 20 to 20. It was Trey's possession.

Trey glanced at the basket, faked a shot, and then went to his left. But Pete was quick. He knocked the ball out of Trey's hand.

Before Trey could react, Pete had grabbed the ball and was running toward the hoop. He made the layup easily and won the game.

"Ha!" Pete shouted.

All the guys watching were laughing and hooting and hollering.

"I won!" Pete yelled. "I beat Trey, one-on-one."

Pete grabbed the ball and dribbled it over to Trey. He was really showing off, doing tricks like dribbling between his legs.

"Whatever," Trey said. He took a swig from his water bottle. "We've been playing all morning."

Pete laughed. "So?" he said.

Trey turned to the other guys watching. "We both won some, we both lost some," he said. "So what if he won that game, right? It was just one game."

Pete came running over. "That was the last game," Pete said. "So that's the one that matters."

Trey turned to his cousin. "Oh yeah?" he said. "Let's see how it goes next week. Westfield will destroy East Lake."

"Oooh," said a few of the guys watching.

Pete glared at his cousin. "We'll see," he said.

"Right, we will," Trey replied. Then he turned and walked off. "I'm going home."

··· Chapter 4 ···
PRACTICE

The rest of the weekend went by quickly. Soon Trey was back at basketball practice with the Wildcats. As shooting guard, it was often Trey's job to get the ball in the hoop. Most plays meant Isaac Roth, the starting point guard, would look for Trey.

That afternoon, Trey, Isaac, and some of the guys from the B team were running drills against the rest of the starters and some other B team players.

Coach T blew his whistle to start the drill. Isaac and Trey and their teammates jogged up the court.

Isaac stopped at the top of the key and Trey cut around to the right. He faked out his defender at the three-point line and caught a perfect pass.

He spun, faked a drive, and shot. Three points!

"Nice shot, Trey," Coach T said. "And nice moves. You really left Dwayne in the dust with that fake."

Dwayne shook his head. "Aw, come on, Coach!" Dwayne said. "I'll get him next time."

The others laughed. Coach T glanced at his watch, and then at the clock over the doors. Then he blew his whistle again.

"That's it for today, gentlemen," he called out. "Hit the showers. Except you, Trey. I want to talk to you."

"Ooh," a few of the other players said. "Trey's in trouble!"

"You getting cut, Trey?" Isaac joked. He hit Trey on the back as he walked past.

"Right," Trey said. "I'm the captain, remember? He just wants to talk to me about how to make sure you don't blow the game for us this week."

Isaac laughed and headed into the locker room. The coach walked over to Trey, carrying his clipboard and flipping through some papers.

"So, this week we play East Lake," Coach Turnbull said. "Any thoughts about the game?"

Trey scratched his head. "Last year we handled them easily," Trey said. "They probably have some good new players, but Joey Hotchsin is in high school now, and so is Paul Birk. Those two were their best players by far."

The coach nodded. "That's true," he said. "But I'm hearing an awful lot about this talented sixth grader named Pete Smith. Ever heard of him?"

"Yes," Trey said quietly. "He's my cousin."

"I thought so," Coach T replied. "Are you two close?"

Trey shrugged. "We play a lot of two-on-two," he said. "Or we used to, anyway. This weekend we played one-on-one, against each other."

"Is Pete a good player?" the coach asked.

Trey shrugged again. "He's all right," he said. For some reason, he didn't feel like bragging about his cousin.

He would have a week before, though. He used to be proud of how good his little cousin was with the ball.

"All right, thanks," the coach said. "And hey, will it be weird playing against him? He's a starter, so you'll be guarding him. And he'll be guarding you."

Trey waved the coach off as he walked toward the locker room. "No worries," Trey assured him. "It will be just like any other game."

··· Chapter 5 ···
SHOWED UP

Just before the game started on Wednesday night, Trey peered out of the locker room door. He spotted his father and Pete's father as they walked into the gym.

The two men talked for a moment at the door. Then, as Trey watched, they went to sit on opposite sides of the court. Trey's dad went to the Wildcats side, while Pete's went to the visitors side.

Then the East Lake team came jogging in to warm up on their end of the court.

Trey spotted his cousin in the front of the East Lake team as they came in. He was waving and smiling at the crowd.

"What a show-off," Trey mumbled.

Dwayne Illy came up next to him. "Who?" he said. "The little guy?"

Trey nodded. "My cousin Pete," he said. "He thinks he's the best basketball player since Michael Jordan."

Dwayne laughed. "He's in sixth grade and he starts?" he asked. "He probably is pretty good, huh?"

The East Lake team started shooting around. Dwayne and Trey watched Pete. He was doing plenty of fancy dribbling and showing off.

"Yeah, he's pretty good all right," Dwayne said.

Then the loudspeaker clicked on. The eighth-grade class president, Tina Hawk, took the microphone. "And now, the Westfield Wildcats!" she announced.

Coach T stood up and clapped as the other four starting Wildcats stood up. Trey groaned and slowly got to his feet.

"Cheer up, Trey," Dwayne said. "We got this game, easy."

Trey nodded and jogged with the other starters out to the court. They lined up for some quick layups. Trey made his shot easily. Then the Wildcats and the East Lake team got ready to play.

The Wildcats got possession first, thanks to PJ Harris, their very tall starting center.

PJ tapped the ball to Isaac Roth. Right away, the Wildcats moved to the basket.

Isaac dribbled at the top of the key. The East Lake player guarding him waited for him to start the play.

Trey watched Isaac as Pete stuck close to him. Pete was all smiles, but Trey was feeling the pressure of a new game. He didn't look Pete in the eye.

Isaac raised three fingers, and Trey faked toward the basket. Then he cut back toward Isaac. He thought he had lost Pete.

Isaac thought so too, so he passed to Trey.

Just then, Pete ran past, knocking the ball away from Trey. Pete quickly dribbled toward the East Lake basket.

Trey tried to get back on defense in time, but Pete was already at the basket.

Pete made the layup easily for the first two points of the game. The score was two to nothing, East Lake.

The crowd on the visitor side cheered and hollered. Someone yelled, "Way to go, Smith!"

It was only a few seconds into the game, and Trey's little cousin had already humiliated him.

··· Chapter 6 ···
BLOWING IT

Trey threw in the ball to Isaac to start play after the first basket.

The coach and Trey's teammates were still in good spirits. Coach Turnbull walked along the sideline, clapping along with the spectators. Trey knew his dad and uncle were both up there, somewhere.

"Look alive out there, guys," Coach T shouted. "Let's make sure that's the last time East Lake steals from us in this game, okay?"

Trey hustled to his spot down the court.

I can't believe I let Pete get that steal, he thought. *Well, I'll show him who the better player is.*

Isaac called a give-and-go, but Trey didn't want to just pass the ball back to Isaac.

Trey wanted to be the one to score the next basket. He had to show Pete he was just as good.

When the pass came, Trey dodged Pete, caught the pass, and went straight to the hoop. With a little fancy dribbling through his legs, Trey went up for the layup.

But too many East Lake players were on him, including Pete. There just wasn't room.

Trey tried to lay the ball up underhanded, but missed. The ball slammed into the bottom of the backboard.

The whole basket shook. Then the ball went flying out of bounds.

"Trey!" Isaac called out. "That was supposed to be a give-and-go. Why'd you drive?"

Trey looked over at the bench. The coach looked angry, and Trey felt like an idiot.

So far, Pete looked like a great player. But Trey had lost a pass and blown a layup.

This game wasn't going well for Trey. Not at all.

East Lake started their possession. Trey hoped their point guard would pass to Pete. That way, Trey would have a chance to make up for his mistakes and show up his cousin at the same time.

But East Lake's point guard glanced toward Pete, then passed to their small forward. East Lake's small forward drove hard to the basket, so Trey fell off Pete and doubled up on the forward.

"Trey!" Coach T called from the sideline. "Get back to your man!"

But it was too late. The East Lake small forward cut his drive short. He passed the ball under his other arm — right to Pete Smith.

Pete was wide open. He casually raised the ball and sank a perfect shot from downtown. Three more points for East Lake!

··· Chapter 7 ···
TALKING TRASH

On Westfield's next possession, Isaac held the ball at the top of the key.

Trey didn't plan to try to show off this time. He'd play it just like he was supposed to. *I'm not going to make that mistake a third time*, he thought.

Finally, Isaac passed to Trey. Trey caught the pass easily, and then faked toward the hoop.

Pete darted alongside to keep up, but Trey stopped short. His sneakers squeaked on the wood floor as he drew up and shot. Two points!

"How's that?" Trey said when Pete turned to face him. "Now who's better?"

Pete smirked at his older cousin and rolled his eyes.

"Nothing to say now, huh?" Trey said.

Pete shook his head and jogged away to start the next possession.

"That's right," Trey called after him. "Walk away. Because you know you got nothing!"

"Trey!" the coach suddenly snapped from the sidelines. "On the bench, right now!" Coach Turnbull was red in the face and out of breath.

Trey swallowed. He didn't like it when the coach was angry.

"Do I need to take you out of this game, Trey?" Coach T asked.

Trey sighed. "No," he said.

"You said it wouldn't be a problem playing against your cousin," Coach Turnbull went on. "But I see now that it is a problem. As a matter of fact, it's looking like a very big problem."

"No, honest, Coach," Trey said. "It's not a problem. I was just kidding around."

The coach just stared at him.

"For real, Coach T," Trey continued. "I just made all those mistakes before, and I was excited to score. That's all."

"Speaking of those mistakes, those weren't like you, Trey," Coach T said. "You're normally a reliable player. You stick to the plan and score points. It's why you're the captain of the team."

"I'm sorry, Coach," Trey said.

The coach sighed. "All right," he said. "You get one more chance out there. No more trash talking, and no more crazy chances. Follow the plan and the Wildcats win, got it?"

"I got it," Trey said. The ref blew the whistle and Trey ran out to join the game.

On defense, Trey stayed calm, but he couldn't stop thinking about how mad Coach Turnbull had been.

The coach never got mad at Trey. Sure, he sometimes hollered at Dwayne Illy for showing off, or at PJ for goofing around during practice. But Trey? He was the team captain.

This is all Pete's fault, Trey thought. *I'll get him back.*

East Lake drove up the court. This time, their forward found their center, who had posted up. But his shot was off.

The rebound came right to Trey. He shoveled it to Isaac and the Westfield fans cheered as they headed back up the court.

Isaac raised a fist as he ran up. Trey followed the play and hustled to his spot just as Pete came up on him.

Now's my chance, Trey thought.

Trey caught the pass, then spun and knocked into Pete. He only hit him with his shoulder, but the ref spotted it. A whistle went off just as Trey laid up the ball for a basket.

"No points," the ref called out. "Charging on Westfield Smith. East Lake Smith will take two shots."

"What?!" Trey shouted at the ref, but Coach T had a hand on his shoulder right away.

"Bench," Coach T said. "Now."

··· **Chapter 8** ···

CHAMPIONSHIP PLAYERS

Trey sat out the rest of the first half. The second string guard couldn't keep up with Pete at all. After a few minutes, East Lake's lead had grown to fifteen points.

Trey knew that his dad and his uncle were looking at him. But he didn't look back at them. He hung his head and stared at the gym floor.

During halftime, the other Wildcats just glared at him.

I know what they're all thinking, Trey thought. *How is this joker the team captain?*

At the moment, Trey wasn't so sure himself. He knew he had screwed up, but he wasn't sure how to fix it.

The coach went over a few plays and corrected a few mistakes. Then he sent the team out to run a few drills. Trey started to follow everyone else.

"Um, hold on a minute, Trey," the coach said. He put a hand on his shoulder.

"Yeah?" Trey said. He turned to face the coach.

Coach T pointed at the locker room bench. "Have a seat," he said.

Trey dropped onto the bench. "Don't you want me to get out there to do drills with the other guys?" Trey asked.

"Trey, I'm not going to start you in the second half," Coach T said.

Trey nodded sadly. "I'm not surprised," he said.

"Until you cool off," the coach went on, "I'm not going to put you back in. Is that clear?"

Trey sighed loudly. "Yeah," he said. "I got it. It's clear."

"All right," the coach said. "Then get out there and hit the wood until you're acting like yourself."

Trey grunted and got to his feet. Then he jogged out of the locker room and went straight to the bench. He sat down next to Daniel Friedland, the second string small forward.

"Hey," Daniel said.

Trey didn't even look at Daniel. He just grunted. He couldn't stop watching Pete, who was on the court, shooting layups with his team.

Just before the second half started, Pete looked over at the Wildcats bench. He and Trey made eye contact, and Pete smiled.

Trey nearly screamed. He couldn't believe Pete was smiling.

Trey wasn't starting. This was all Pete's fault, and Pete had the nerve to laugh about it!

"Hi, son," a voice suddenly said.

Trey turned around. His father and Pete's father were standing behind him.

"Oh hi, Dad," Trey said. "Hi, Uncle Theo. Enjoying the game?"

"No, we're not, Trey," Dad replied. He wasn't smiling.

Trey looked at his feet.

"You know, Trey," Uncle Theo said, "when your father and I were in college, basketball wasn't our game."

"So?" Trey said.

"We played baseball," Uncle Theo went on. "And since we're close in age and went to different colleges, we played each other a few times."

Dad's face suddenly lit up. "Remember that one game, Theo?" he said.

Uncle Theo nodded. "Sure," he said. "The championship, senior year. Biggest game I ever played in."

"Trey, I wish you could have seen it," Dad said. "It was the old classic scenario. The bottom of the ninth inning . . ."

"Two outs," Uncle Theo put in. "And I was pitching to the best hitter at State."

"Me!" Dad said. "We were down by two runs. There were two men on base, and I was up. The pressure was on."

"And hey," Uncle Theo said. "I was a good pitcher, don't forget."

"Best in the league," Trey's dad admitted.

"A hush fell over the stands," Uncle Theo said. "The whole stadium was on the edge of their seats."

"What pitch did you throw?" Trey's dad asked. "Was it a slider?"

"Nope. Breaking fastball," Uncle Theo said. "I had a great breaking pitch."

Neither man said anything for a few moments. Trey heard the ref blow his whistle to get the basketball players ready for the second half.

"So?" Trey said finally. "Who won the championship?"

The two men looked at each other. Then they burst out laughing.

"That's the thing, Trey," his father said.

"We can never remember!" Uncle Theo finished.

The two men laughed again. Then Trey's father looked at him.

"Get the idea, son?" Dad asked seriously.

Trey nodded. "Yeah," he said. "I get the idea."

··· Chapter 9 ···
WHO WON?

The second half began. Trey tapped the coach on the shoulder.

"Hey, Coach T," Trey said. "I'm sorry for acting like such a jerk in the first half. I'm cooled off now. I'd like to play."

The coach looked at Trey for a long moment. "All right," he said. "Next stop in play, you're going in. Don't make me regret this decision."

After a few moments, the whistle blew. The coach patted Trey on the back, so he jogged onto the court to replace the second-string shooting guard.

"Hey, cuz," Pete said when Trey came up to him.

"Hey, Pete," Trey replied. He put out his hand. "No hard feelings?"

Pete shook his cousin's hand. "Of course not," he said. "We going to play some basketball now?"

"Definitely," Trey said. Both cousins smiled as play began again.

Isaac Roth got the ball to Trey right away. Trey faked a drive, then drew up and shot from behind the three-point line.

"Yes," he said as the shot fell. He heard the crowd cheering for him.

"Nice shot," Pete said.

East Lake's point guard got the ball to Pete. After a pump that left Trey faked out, Pete drove to the hoop.

Trey recovered quickly and caught up to his cousin. With a burst of speed, he was able to knock the ball away from Pete and out of bounds.

"East Lake ball," the ref called out. He handed the ball to East Lake's point guard to throw in.

The point guard found Pete again right away. This time, Pete faked the drive and took a quick shot for two points. Trey was totally fooled.

"Wow," Trey said. "You really got me that time, little cousin."

"Plenty of time left in the half," Pete said.

Trey smiled as the two of them headed back up court. "You know it," he said.

··· Chapter 10 ···
TWO-ON-TWO

At the park the next weekend, Pete and Trey were playing two-on-two against a couple of guys from Josette. They'd already won three games that morning, and it wasn't even lunchtime yet.

"Right here, cuz," Trey called to Pete.

"Get open!" Pete called back.

The player from Josette was taller than Pete, and he had him stopped.

Trey spun to his left, then darted across the key. His defender tripped up and Pete found Trey with a fast pass. Trey laid it up for the game-winning point.

"All right!" Pete said. The cousins high-fived at the foul line.

"Any more takers?" Pete said to some other kids watching. No one replied.

"That's fine," Uncle Theo said, walking over. "It's time for lunch anyway."

"We've got burgers and chicken," Dad added, "hot off the grill."

Trey picked up the basketball. Then he and Pete jogged over to the picnic table. One of the boys from Josette called over to them as they were about to eat.

"Hey, you two!" the kid said. "Don't you two go to Westfield and East Lake?"

"Yeah," Trey replied. "So?"

"Well, didn't your teams play each other this week?" the Josette boy asked.

"Yes," Pete called back.

"So who won?" the boy said.

Trey and Pete looked at their dads, then at each other. They turned to the boy from Josette and replied together with a shrug, "We don't remember!"

13 PJ HARRIS
WILDCATS

WILDCATS

Wildcat

Scoring/Shooting

#	Athlete Name	Position	PPG	FT %	FG %	Stl	Reb
6	Danny Powell	Center	9	73.2	82.8	5	22
11	Daniel Friedland	Forward	5.7	95.8	85.1	12	10
13	PJ Harris	Center	22	65.6	90.2	7	32
23	Trey Smith Ⓒ	Guard	14	96.2	80.5	20	8
26	Isaac Roth	Guard	11.5	94.1	79.3	11	6
33	Dwayne Illy	Forward	6.2	82.9	77.9	9	13

Athlete Highlight: **PJ Harris**

13

TABLE OF CONTENTS

JUST PRACTICE

PJ Harris looked down at his shoes, size 13.
He was the tallest guy on the Wildcats basketball
team, and his feet were the longest. But he wasn't
thinking about his feet, or his height. He was
thinking about the foul line.

He looked up. The basket hung ten feet high,
thirteen feet away. Down both sides of the lane,
players stood in red or yellow jerseys, watching
him out of the corners of their eyes as they looked
up at the basket.

PJ looked down at his yellow jersey, then at
the ball, and took a deep breath. His heart was
pounding. He could hear the voices of people
watching, cheering him on or taunting him.

He looked up at the basket, pulled the ball back over his shoulder with both hands, and shot.

Brick!

The whole backboard shook as the ball slammed into the rim, then fell right back to the wood. It bounced hard into the lane, and one of PJ's opponents grabbed the rebound. In seconds, it was back up the court, and the other team had scored.

A whistle blew and PJ shook his head. "Scrimmage over," the coach called out. "Red jerseys win."

It was only practice, but PJ felt awful. "Man, why can't I ever make a foul shot?" he muttered to himself.

Dwayne Illy, the starting small forward, heard him. "What did you say?" he asked.

PJ turned and said, "Oh, nothing. No big deal. I missed the foul shot. It's just practice, right?" He laughed and gave Dwayne a high five.

"Practice is where we improve, PJ," Coach Turnbull said. "If you'd stop goofing around when you miss those foul shots, maybe you'd improve."

"I know, Coach T," PJ replied. "I'm not goofing around."

I'm only laughing so I don't look stupid, he thought, but he didn't want to explain that to Coach Turnbull.

"Don't even worry about it," Dwayne said. "Who cares about a center shooting foul shots?"

"Yeah, that's your job," PJ said, smiling. "You take most of the foul shots, 'cause you get fouled a lot."

"That's right," Dwayne said. "And I have the best foul shot on this team. So no worries, right?"

PJ laughed. "How many foul shots do I even take a season?" he said. "Like four?"

Dwayne nodded. "Maybe two!" he said. The two boys laughed and joined the rest of the team for layup drills.

••• Chapter 2 •••
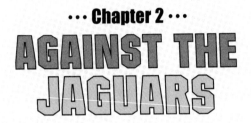
AGAINST THE JAGUARS

The next day was Thursday — game day. The Wildcats took on the Grayson City Jaguars.

The referee tossed the ball up and PJ jumped. He knocked the ball toward Dwayne. The Westfield side of the stands cheered. PJ was feeling good. He ran up the court and took his spot at the bottom of the lane. The other team's center was guarding him very closely. *Too closely*, PJ thought.

The Jaguars center elbowed PJ as he moved across the baseline. "Watch it," PJ said. He used his arm to box out the other player when Trey put up a three-point attempt.

The shot missed. PJ jumped up. He grabbed the rebound and laid it back up for two points.

"Nice job, Harris," Coach Turnbull called out. He clapped a couple of times. "Way to get in there. Keep boxing that guy out!"

PJ ran up the court and picked up the other center on defense. When the Jaguars small forward moved down the lane, faked a shot, and tossed the ball to the center, PJ was right there. He put up a hand and easily blocked the layup.

The Jaguars center fell on his butt in the paint. The ref blew his whistle to stop play.

PJ tried to help the other player up. "Hey, man," PJ said, "sorry about that."

But the Jaguars center just smacked his hand away. "I'm fine," he snapped. He got to his feet.

It was a tight first half, and PJ worked hard for every rebound. He blocked a couple more shots — including two more layup attempts by the Jaguars center.

When the buzzer sounded, the Wildcats were up by only two points. PJ watched as the Jaguars center stormed off the court.

··· Chapter 4 ···

PLAY HARD

Right before the start of the second half, Coach Turnbull stood in front of his team's bench. The players were all seated or standing around.

"Great job in the first half, guys," the coach said. "Dwayne, how are you feeling? Up for starting the second half?"

"I feel great, Coach T," Dwayne replied. "Man, I could play these fools into the ground all day." He laughed.

"I know it," the coach said. "Same five, then. Huddle up."

The five starters stood around the coach and leaned in.

"On three, 'Wildcats,'" the coach said. "One, two, three . . ."

And the five starters shouted: "Wildcats!"

The huddle broke, and the guys took the court.

"Just a second, Harris," Coach Turnbull said.

PJ turned around and jogged back to the coach. "Don't you want me in again, Coach?" PJ asked.

The coach nodded. "Of course," he said. "Your hustle is great today. You're really giving that Jaguars center a hard time."

"Thanks, Coach T," PJ said.

"Just be careful. Don't be too rough," the coach added. "I don't want you to get in trouble out there."

PJ nodded. "You got it, Coach," he said. Then he went to the sideline.

The ref blew his whistle, then handed the Jaguars center the ball. The Jaguars center threw it in to one of his teammates.

No matter what PJ did, he couldn't reach the ball.

The fans in the visitor bleachers cheered. PJ shook his head and ran up the court. He picked up his man at the baseline and tried to keep him out of rebound position.

The Jaguars shooting guard took a shot from just inside the three-point line, and it swished. No rebound required. The game was tied.

The second half was tiring. PJ's man was playing very hard and very rough.

While PJ played, he watched his teammates. Each of them was playing his hardest. Every point they scored was fought for, and every drive they stopped was even tougher.

As the clock ticked down, the score stayed painfully close. With only a few seconds left on the clock, the Wildcats were down by one point.

Isaac Roth, a Wildcats point guard, held the ball for an instant at the top of the key. PJ stepped in front of his defender and cut hard under the basket.

It was just enough time for Isaac to connect with PJ, who caught the pass on the way up to the basket.

Suddenly he felt a strong arm across his throat and shoulders. The next thing he knew, the ball was bouncing slowly toward the bleachers, and his butt was on the wood.

A whistle blew. "That's two," the ref shouted.

PJ looked up at the scoreboard. The Wildcats were still down by one, and he had two chances to tie it up, or even win.

··· Chapter 4 ···

CHOKE

PJ stood at the foul line. He held the ball under one arm and looked up at the basket. His hands were sweaty. PJ wasn't sure if it was from the tough game, or his nervousness.

Coach Turnbull called out from the bench, "You got these, Harris. We only need one for the tie."

"Come on, PJ!" the players called from the bench.

A hand slapped his back. "All you, Harris," Dwayne said from behind him.

In front of PJ, Wildcats and Jaguars lined up, waiting for his shot.

From the bleachers, he heard classmates shouting, "PJ! PJ! PJ!"

From the other side, some students from Grayson City called out, too. "Boo! Choke!"

PJ tried to ignore them, but his heart pounded and his hands shook. Finally he looked up at the basket, pulled back his arms, and shot.

Right away, he knew it was an air ball. The ball arced too soon and dropped at least six inches short of the rim.

The ref handed the ball back to him for his second shot.

"That's okay," the coach called out, clapping. "You've got another shot, and we only need one point to enter overtime."

PJ's mouth felt dry. He squinted through the sweat in his eyes, drew back the ball, and shot.

This time it wasn't even close. The ball slammed into the backboard and dropped right into the hands of the Jaguars power forward. He grabbed the ball, drove it quickly up the court, right past Dwayne, and laid it up for another two points. Then the buzzer went off.

The ref blew his whistle. He called out, "Game over."

PJ looked at the gym ceiling and shook his head. He muttered to himself, "Life over."

··· Chapter 5 ···

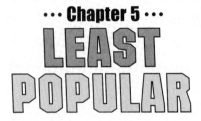

LEAST POPULAR

When Friday morning's alarm buzzed next to PJ's head, he groaned.

"Up and at 'em, PJ," his dad called from the kitchen.

But PJ was all out of energy that morning, and not just because the game the night before had left him exhausted. He also knew he'd have to face an entire school's worth of angry people.

He had blown the game against Grayson City Middle School, and everyone knew it. He wouldn't be surprised if the principal mentioned it on the morning announcements during homeroom, just in case anyone had missed the game.

"Come on, Peter Joseph," Dad called, more sternly. "Unless you want to walk in the rain, you better get moving. I have to leave for the shop in fifteen minutes, and you're not skipping breakfast."

PJ got to his feet and rubbed his eyes. Then he got dressed in the clothes he thought would attract the least attention. Of course, when you're fourteen years old, but five feet and ten inches tall, people tend to notice you no matter what you wear.

PJ walked into the kitchen. "Morning," he mumbled.

"Why the long face?" Dad asked.

"I blew the game last night," PJ said. "Because of me and my awful foul shots, we lost to Grayson City."

Dad frowned. "Ouch," he said. "They're one of Westfield's biggest rivals."

"No kidding," PJ said sadly.

"I doubt it was really your fault," Dad said. "There are five guys on the court at a time, right? They all made a difference, win or lose."

PJ shook his head. "You don't understand," he said. He went to the fridge and took a swig of OJ from the carton.

"I'm pretending I didn't see that because you're in a bad mood," Dad said. "Eat fast. You have ten minutes."

* * *

At school, PJ kept his head down. There was no announcement about PJ blowing the game, of course, but they did announce the final score. A few people in PJ's homeroom, including Dwayne, glared at him during the announcement.

PJ dropped his head onto his desk. He kept his head on his desk until the buzzer rang and everyone else left.

When he picked his head up, Dwayne was standing next to him.

"Oh, uh," PJ stammered. "Hi, Dwayne."

"I can't believe you showed your face today," Dwayne said.

PJ leaned back in his chair and looked up at the ceiling. He sighed. "It wasn't all my fault we lost, you know," he mumbled.

"Oh really?" Dwayne said. "Was there someone else up at that foul line shooting bricks and air balls?"

"We all played the game, Dwayne," PJ replied. "If you had scored more baskets during regulation play, we would have won. Maybe it was your fault."

"What?" Dwayne snapped.

PJ shrugged. "I'm just saying," he said. "I'm not trying to blame you."

Dwayne took a deep breath. "All right," he said. "However you want to break it down, PJ, the whole school is mad at you right now."

"I know," PJ said. "I was thinking about asking for your help. After school. Meet me at the outside court?"

Dwayne nodded. "Yeah, all right," he said, backing out of the room. "I'll see you, PJ. Keep your head down today."

PJ heard him laughing as he walked away.

··· Chapter 6 ···
LESSONS?

As PJ pushed through the back doors of the school that afternoon, he could feel the other students' stares like laser beams. But then he heard the rubber echo of a basketball not far off, and he felt a little better.

PJ went around to the north side of the school. There was Dwayne, dribbling the basketball, and sinking shots from the outside.

Dwayne looked up and saw PJ, then did some trick dribbling, drove on the hoop, and laid it up.

"Nice one," PJ said, walking up.

"Yeah," Dwayne replied. He took the ball up to the free-throw line. "Now, first lesson. Watch the master."

PJ went over to the baseline and stood under the backboard. Dwayne stood at the line, pulled the ball back over his shoulder, and in one smooth motion took the shot.

Swish!

It was perfect.

PJ caught the ball off one bounce. He started heading to the free-throw line.

"Not yet, PJ," Dwayne said, holding his hands out. "Toss it back."

PJ stopped in the key and shrugged. "All right," he said. He passed the ball back.

"You need to study my form a little more," Dwayne explained. He looked up at the basket and let another shot fly. It went in off the backboard.

This time, the rebound rolled back to Dwayne. He scooped up the ball and lined up another shot.

PJ stood at the baseline and watched as Dwayne took shot after shot. Every time PJ got a rebound, Dwayne told him to give the ball to him one more time.

"Hey, Dwayne," PJ said. "Think maybe I should take a few shots if I want to get any better?"

Dwayne hushed him and took another perfect foul shot. "I think for your first lesson," he said, "you should just watch the master."

PJ waved him off. "Man, I've seen you shoot about a thousand free throws before I came out here today," he said.

Dwayne laughed and took another shot. "And you still can't shoot," he said. "So you better keep watching."

PJ shook his head. "This is ridiculous," he muttered. Then he walked off toward the bus stop.

Dwayne called after him, "You'll never learn!"

PJ mumbled under his breath, "Not from you, anyway."

··· Chapter 7 ···
PRACTICE!

Monday couldn't have come soon enough. Normally PJ loved the weekends, but this weekend was different.

He didn't want to see any of his friends from the team, since they all probably still hated him. And he couldn't go down to the park courts to practice because it rained Saturday morning to Sunday night.

Early Monday morning, PJ walked down the quiet halls of Westfield Middle School toward Coach Turnbull's office.

The office door stood open, so PJ reached in and knocked on it. "Hey, Coach T?" he said nervously.

"Oh, Harris," Coach Turnbull said. He was sitting as his desk, sipping coffee out of a mug that said *I Love Dogs.* "Come on in."

"Do you hate me as much as the rest of the team does, Coach T?" PJ asked. He sat down.

The coach put down his mug. "Hate you?" he asked. "What are you talking about, Harris?"

"You know," PJ replied. He didn't look the coach in the eye. "Because I lost the game for us."

"Lost the game?" the coach said. "That's crazy. You missed a couple of foul shots. Lots of guys missed shots."

PJ shrugged. "I guess," he said.

"Listen, Harris," the coach went on, "you didn't lose the game for us, but you should work on your foul shot. Why don't you talk to Dwayne? He's got a great free throw."

"I don't think so," PJ said. "Any other ideas?"

"Well, there's Daniel Friedland," the coach said. He looked through some papers on his clipboard. "His foul shot has really improved over the last season. I think he's gunning for the starting five at Dwayne's position."

PJ thought about it. He had noticed Daniel's shots improving a lot, even though he hardly ever played in a game.

"Okay, Coach," PJ said, getting up. "I'll find Daniel and ask for some tips."

"I'm glad you're trying to improve that shot, PJ," the coach said.

* * *

Daniel Friedland was in PJ's math class. PJ went over to him just before class started.

"Hey, PJ," Daniel replied. "Bummer about that game last week, huh?"

"Yeah," PJ said. "At least you're still talking to me."

"I don't think anyone's mad at you about it," Daniel said. "At least not anymore."

PJ said, "I was hoping you could give me some tips. I know your free throw has gotten a lot better since last season."

"Wait a second. You noticed that?" Daniel said excitedly.

"Sure," PJ replied. "So did Coach T. He said I should ask you for some tips."

Daniel smiled. "Wow," he said. He got a faraway look on his face. "You think Coach T will let me start soon?"

"Come on, Daniel, focus," PJ said. "How did you get better?"

Daniel looked at PJ. "Huh?" he said. "Oh! Right. Well, I just practice. A lot! Like, every morning before school, I spend thirty minutes at the park courts, just shooting foul shot after foul shot."

PJ's eyes opened wide. "Every morning?" he said. "That's insane. What time do you get up every day?"

Daniel shrugged. "Six. It's no big deal," he explained. "My mom makes me breakfast and I head to the park."

The bell rang to start class, so PJ slid into his seat at the back of the room.

Every morning? he thought. *And at six? That's so early. I don't know if I can do that.*

* * *

The next morning, PJ's alarm went off at six. Somehow, he managed to pull himself out of bed.

He threw on some sweats and a hoodie, then some socks he found that didn't seem too dirty.

"What are you doing up already?" his dad said when PJ reached the front door.

"I'm going to shoot some free throws at the park," PJ said. He pulled on his basketball shoes. "I need to improve my shot if I don't want to lose any more games for the Wildcats."

When PJ made it to the park courts, the first thing he saw was Daniel Friedland, shooting from the foul line.

"Hey, you made it," Daniel called out. "Nice."

PJ said, "I guess I'll use the other basket."

Daniel nodded, then went right back to shooting free throws.

Man, he's so serious about it, PJ thought. Then he went to the other basket and stood at the foul line.

PJ yawned. He glanced at his watch. It was only six thirty. School wouldn't start for another hour and a half.

That leaves plenty of time to practice, he thought. *If I can stay awake.*

PJ glanced over at Daniel. He wasn't as good as Dwayne from the line, but he was sinking most of his shots.

PJ looked back at his own basket, then at his ball. He took a deep breath, spun the ball between his palms, and lifted it up. He aimed. And all he could think about was Daniel, behind him, watching him.

PJ took another deep breath, drew the ball back, and shot.

Brick.

The ball slammed into the metal rim with a thud, shaking the backboard and the pole. Then it bounced right back at him, over his head, and onto Daniel's side of the court.

"Aw, man!" PJ shouted.

Daniel caught PJ's ball and tossed it back. "No big deal," he said. "Keep going."

PJ glared at Daniel, who smiled and went back to practicing.

PJ stood, facing his own basket, listening to the sounds behind him: the ball bouncing once or twice. Then silence.

Then he'd hear the ball hitting the rim and falling in, or hitting the backboard and falling in. Then the ball would bounce another couple of times and PJ would hear Daniel's feet on the cement.

PJ's heart raced. The sun was behind his hoop, and he squinted toward the basket. After a deep breath, he bounced the ball once, lifted it up, and shot.

The ball came off his fingers all wrong. There was no arc, and no power. It fell at least six inches short of the front of the rim and rolled onto the grass.

"No!" PJ shouted. Then he walked off.

"PJ?" Daniel called after him. "What about your ball? PJ?"

But PJ ignored him. He had one option left, and that was to quit the team.

··· Chapter 8 ···
QUITTER

PJ still had an hour before school started, so he decided to head home and have breakfast.

Then he'd go to school, find Coach T, and quit the basketball team.

"Back already?" PJ's dad asked when PJ walked into their apartment. "You can't have gotten much practicing done."

"It was a waste of time," PJ said.

He kept moving right through the living room, down the hall, and into his bedroom. There, he flopped onto his bed.

Dad followed him. "What's going on?" he asked.

"I'm going to quit the basketball team," PJ said. Then he picked up a stuffed mini basketball from his bed and shot it at the trashcan across the room. It went in.

"Quitting the team?" Dad repeated, shocked.

"Don't get mad," PJ said. "I can't shoot a foul shot to save my life. All I'm good at is being tall."

"That's nonsense," Dad said. "You're great at getting those rebounds, and I've seen your shot. It's good! And you love basketball!"

"My shot is good?" PJ said. "You should have seen me this morning at the courts. A brick and an airball. It was a really great show. Daniel Friedland is probably still down there, rolling on the cement with laughter."

"I doubt that," Dad replied. "What was he doing down there at this hour anyway?"

PJ explained how Daniel had gotten so much better this season by practicing every morning.

As he talked, he got up from the bed and grabbed the stuffed basketball out of the trash. Then he sat down on the bed's edge again and shot the ball again. Again, it went in.

"So maybe you should do the same as him," Dad suggested.

"That was my plan," PJ said, "but with Daniel right there, I got so nervous."

"Because Daniel might be watching you?" Dad asked. He sat next to PJ on the edge of the bed.

PJ shrugged. "I guess," he said. "I don't know what to do about it. My heart races, I can't take a deep breath, and my hands sweat. Plus, now the whole team hates me. That makes it even worse!"

"I get nervous too," Dad said. "At the shop, I sometimes get so frustrated when I can't get a cut just right, or when I start assembling pieces and the whole shop is noisy and I can't concentrate."

"Dad, basketball and carpentry have nothing to do with each other," PJ said, rolling his eyes.

"Just hear me out," Dad said. "When the shop is like that, and I just can't think straight, and the piece isn't coming together like I need it to, sometimes I just want to take whatever I'm working on and throw it at the wall. Just forget about it."

"So do you?" PJ asked.

Dad smiled at PJ. "No way. I can't do that," Dad said.

"Why not?" PJ asked.

"Well," Dad explained, "because this is for some customer who needs his new dining room table, or kitchen cabinets, or whatever. So I take a deep breath, and I close my eyes. And in my mind I picture the pieces going together perfectly. I go over the whole thing in my head, so everything fits just like I measured it."

"And?" PJ said.

"And before you know it," Dad said, smiling, "I can't even hear the other guys in the shop. The machines are quiet, like they're miles away. I take a deep, calm breath, and get back to work. Then it always works out."

PJ lay back on the bed and thought about what his father had said. Maybe he was right.

Maybe they both got nervous. Maybe the same thing that worked for Dad would work for PJ.

··· Chapter 9 ···
GAME DAY

PJ didn't quit the basketball team when he got to school on Tuesday, but during practice that afternoon, he wished he had. He managed to sink a couple of shots, but he still felt really nervous with everyone watching him.

When game day came around on Thursday, he was sure the coach would keep him benched. But he was wrong. He started, like he always did.

"Are you sure, Coach T?" PJ asked as the other four starters got on the court. "I've been messing up a lot."

"I'm sure," the coach said. "Get out there."

PJ shrugged and went to center court for the jump ball.

The ref blew his whistle, then tossed the ball up. PJ was much taller than the center from East Harrington, so he won the jump easily. He got his whole hand on the ball and knocked it right to Isaac, the point guard. Then PJ ran up the court as fast as he could and took his place at the bottom of the key.

Isaac held up two fingers on his right hand, then cut to his left. PJ knew that hand signal meant he would look for Dwayne at the top of the key.

PJ moved to the top of the lane to set up a pick just as Dwayne caught the pass and started to drive toward the hoop. PJ stood right in the way of Dwayne's defender and Dwayne made the layup easily. The score was 2-0, Wildcats.

The whole first half went well. PJ got a lot of rebounds, and scored eight points from the floor. When the second half started, the Wildcats were up by ten points.

In the second half, PJ quickly got the ball. He passed it to Isaac, but then everything started going wrong.

Isaac tried to find Dwayne when he cut across the key, but the pass was blocked. When the East Harrington player started driving quickly back down the court, Isaac chased him on defense.

Under the Wildcats basket, Isaac jumped to try to block the East Harrington player's layup, but he didn't reach it. Instead he landed on his side, out of bounds. The coach and the school nurse ran over to him.

"It's not serious," the nurse said, "but it will be a nasty bruise. He should sit out the rest of the game."

The coach sighed and waved to the bench. The second-string point guard would have to go in and play.

From then on, the Wildcats really had to struggle. PJ worked hard under the boards and got a few rebounds, but several plays fell apart. The second-string point guard didn't know them as well, and his passes weren't quite as smooth as Isaac's usually were.

With only a few seconds left, the Wildcats were down by one point.

Dwayne Illy took a hard drive through three defenders. The ball got knocked out of his hand, and right into PJ's, under the basket.

PJ pumped once, then jumped up and tried to lay the ball in. But two defenders came down on his arm and knocked him to the wood.

The whistle blew.

PJ's heart nearly stopped. His team was down by one, and he was about to go to the line. Again!

··· Chapter 10 ···
AT THE LINE

PJ was sweating. He wiped some sweat off his face, then looked up at the game clock. There was less than one second left.

The defenders and PJ's teammates lined up on both sides of the lane. They all watched him.

The ref handed him the basketball, and PJ spun it between his palms.

PJ looked at his teammates. Dwayne looked at the floor and shook his head. Isaac Roth, with a wrap on his knee, sighed and looked away. Daniel Friedland tried to smile, but he looked nervous. Trey Smith, their captain, winked at PJ, but didn't smile.

Coach Turnbull clapped and shouted, "You can do this, Harris. We only need one to tie. We can win it in OT!"

PJ looked up at the stands. His dad was in the back row of the bleachers. He looked right at PJ, then closed his eyes, and smiled.

PJ shrugged. It was a worth a try. So he closed his eyes. In his mind, he pictured himself shooting. The ball left his hands smoothly and sailed perfectly toward the basket. It felt right coming off his fingers. In his mind, it was a perfect swish.

After a few seconds, PJ couldn't hear the coach, or the cheering and booing from the bleachers. It was as if he was alone in the gym.

PJ held the ball in his hands and lifted it up to aim. Then he opened his eyes. He felt himself smiling, and he shot.

Swish!

The whole gym went crazy. Everyone from Westfield jumped at the same time. The other Wildcats leaped up from the bench and cheered for PJ.

Coach Turnbull shouted, "Great shot, Harris! You tied it up. No pressure at all now. Just take a nice shot. Either way, we got these guys in OT!"

PJ looked at the coach and nodded, then looked at his dad and smiled. His dad gave him a thumbs-up.

PJ looked back at the basket. This time it was easy. He closed his eyes a moment, took a deep breath, and shot. Off the backboard, the ball dropped for the second point.

As the ball fell through the hoop and bounced onto the wood, the Wildcats players and their fans jumped up again. They swarmed the court, cheering for PJ. PJ couldn't believe it. The Wildcats had won!

"I guess watching me shoot really helped, huh?" Dwayne said. PJ rolled his eyes.

"Did you find a different court to practice that shot on?" Daniel Friedland asked. "I haven't seen you at the park since Tuesday morning."

PJ laughed and shook his head. "Nope," he explained. "I had it in me all along. I just didn't know it till my dad showed me where it was."

11

DANIEL FRIEDLAND

WILDCATS

WILDCATS

Scoring/Shooting

#	Athlete Name	Position	PPG	FT %	FG %	Stl	Reb
6	Danny Powell	Center	9	73.2	82.8	5	22
11	Daniel Friedland	Forward	5.7	95.8	85.1	12	10
13	PJ Harris	Center	22	65.6	90.2	7	32
23	Trey Smith ⓒ	Guard	14	96.2	80.5	20	8
26	Isaac Roth	Guard	11.5	94.1	79.3	11	6
33	Dwayne Illy	Forward	6.2	82.9	77.9	9	13

Athlete Highlight: **Daniel Friedland**

11

OFF THE BENCH
TABLE OF CONTENTS

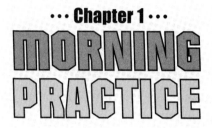

MORNING PRACTICE

Daniel Friedland looked down at his sneakers. He inched up until his toes were close to the foul line, painted in white on the blacktop. He held his basketball in front of him and spun it between his palms. When he took a deep breath, the air was cold and his nose stung.

Slowly, he breathed out through his mouth. He looked at the basket through the cloud of vapor.

Then he pulled back the ball and shot.

Swish!

Daniel let himself smile. After months of coming down to the public courts every morning to practice his foul shot, he rarely missed.

Daniel pulled up the zipper of his hooded sweatshirt. It was still very cold this early in the morning. The bell to begin homeroom over at Westfield Middle School wouldn't ring for another hour.

He jogged over to the basket and grabbed the ball before it rolled onto the grass. Then he quickly walked back to the foul line.

"I think I'm as good as Dwayne Illy now," Daniel muttered to himself. "At least from the foul line."

Dwayne Illy was the starting small forward and the top scorer on the team. Most of his points, though, were from the foul line.

Daniel lifted the ball to take another shot. "If I'm ever going to start at small forward," he said to himself, "I need to be better from the line than Dwayne."

Daniel released the ball.

Swish!

He jogged to the basket and grabbed the ball as it dropped from the hoop. Quickly, he jumped up and went for a layup.

The ball hit the corner of the rim and the backboard and fell back to the blacktop.

Daniel's shoulders sagged.

"Aw, who am I kidding?" Daniel muttered. "Coach T will never start me, not with Dwayne Illy on the team."

Dejected, he put the ball under his arm and headed home to shower before school.

··· Chapter 2 ···

Later that week, Daniel sat on the bench as the Wildcats played the Hornets from Josette Junior High. The first half had been very close, so Coach T started the five top players in the second.

That meant not Daniel.

Dwayne Illy drove hard to the basket and was fouled. From the line he got two points. The second half was starting just how the coach wanted.

On the next drive, Isaac Roth, starting point guard, stopped at the top of the key. He pumped once to fake a shot.

The Hornets defender was fooled, and Isaac got a clear pass to Dwayne as he drove the lane.

Dwayne caught the pass and laid up the ball in one motion. It was smooth.

All five starters high-fived and cheered. Daniel did his best to cheer too, but it was hard to be excited when he was spending the whole game on the bench.

The rest of the second half went just as well. Dwayne Illy got sixteen more points from the line and six from the floor.

With two minutes left in the game, the Westfield Wildcats were up by twenty points.

"All right, you guys," Coach T said to the five players on the bench, including Daniel. "Here's your chance to shine."

The five starters took a seat on the bench, and the five second-string players took the court. Daniel could tell that the other guys weren't very excited. They all knew the coach only played them when the Wildcats had the game in the bag.

"Guys," Daniel said to the other second-stringers. "Let's make the most of this."

"What do you mean?" asked Sam Yohai, the point guard.

"All we have to do is wind the clock down, right?" Daniel asked. "Well, I think we should put a few points up there. Let's show Coach T that we're as good as those starters."

Sam looked at Daniel and the other second-stringers. "But," he said slowly, "we're not."

Daniel rolled his eyes. "Listen," he said, "just get me the ball one time so I can drive. Come on. You'll see."

Play started, and Sam called a play from the top of the key. Daniel cut across the key, caught Sam's pass, and drove for the hoop.

Daniel's defender gave him enough space, and Daniel went for the layup.

Brick!

With a thud, the ball slapped into the bottom of the rim and fell hard, right into the hands of the Hornets center. He heaved the ball up the court to the Hornets star player, who scored right away.

"All right, guys," Coach T called. He looked right at Daniel. "That's enough showing off out there. Just hold the lead, okay?"

Daniel sighed. *Great*, he thought. *This was my chance, and I messed it up.*

"See?" Sam said. "Let's just finish this."

Daniel shook his head. "I guess this is why we're second-string," he mumbled.

··· Chapter 3 ···
STARTING?

"From one bench to another bench," Daniel muttered. He was sitting on the plank of wood, held up by two iron posts, in front of his locker after the game. He sighed.

"Talking to yourself again, Friedland?" Dwayne Illy said. Daniel hadn't noticed him walking by.

"What?" Daniel said. "Oh, no, I'm just, um, thinking."

"None of my business," Dwayne said, stopping him. Then he walked into Coach Turnbull's office.

"I really have to stop talking to myself," Daniel said quietly. He reached into his locker for his street clothes.

No need to shower, he thought. *One drive to the hoop isn't enough for me to break a sweat.*

As he pulled off his team jersey, he overheard Dwayne and the coach talking.

"All week?" the coach said. "That means you'll miss our game against Killcreek!"

"I know, Coach T," Dwayne replied. "But I can't do anything about it. The whole family is going to visit my aunt in Arlington. It's the annual Illy family reunion."

The coach sighed loudly. "I don't like this at all, Dwayne. Can't your whole family wait until school vacation, like everyone else?" Coach T said.

"Last year, my cousins missed school, but our school was on break," Dwayne explained. "This year, it's my turn. Our school schedules are different."

The coach's chair creaked. "Well, it can't be helped," Coach Turnbull said. "I guess we can survive one week without the great Dwayne Illy."

Dwayne laughed. "I don't know about that," he said.

Daniel heard the coach's door close. He pulled on his shirt and acted like he hadn't been listening. When Dwayne walked by, Daniel didn't even look at him.

Once Dwayne was out of earshot, Daniel dropped back onto the bench. "Well," he muttered, "maybe I'll get to start at small forward after all."

He grabbed his jeans from his locker. "Of course, with the way I drove today," he added, "I'm not so sure I want to."

··· **Chapter 4** ···

Daniel decided to walk home from school that day. He usually rode the late bus, but it was a nice afternoon, and the bus was always loud. The walk would give him some time to think.

The walk home wasn't very long. Daniel practiced his dribbling skills as he walked, sometimes just bouncing his ball at his side, sometimes switching hands suddenly, through his legs.

When Daniel reached his house, he stopped in the driveway and continued to practice his dribbling. A few minutes later, he heard a car horn and looked up. His dad was waiting to drive into the driveway.

"Hi, Dad," Daniel called out. He moved to the side to let his father park.

The old car's brakes squeaked as it stopped. The door creaked as Dad climbed out. "I hope you finished your homework," Dad said. "Otherwise I know you wouldn't be out here playing ball."

"Actually, I just got home," Daniel replied. He stopped dribbling and held the ball under his arm. "I decided to walk home today."

Together, Daniel and his father headed up the sidewalk and into the house.

Inside, Dad grabbed the mail off the floor just inside the door. As he flipped through it, he said, "Something on your mind?"

Daniel dropped his sweatshirt and basketball in the front closet. "Yes," he said. "You know Dwayne Illy?"

"Do I know Dwayne?" Dad repeated. "Of course I do. He's the one who's been keeping my son on the bench. What about him?"

"Well, he'll be on vacation for our next game," Daniel replied. "So I think I'll be starting at small forward against Killcreek."

Dad smiled. "That's great, Danny," he said. "This is your chance to show that coach what you're made of, what you can do out there!"

"Um, it sure is," Daniel said. He hadn't meant to keep anything from his father, but he couldn't tell him how bad he was at driving the lane. Or about how he'd missed his one chance to score during the game.

"So, that's all I wanted to tell you," Daniel said, going for the stairs. "I better get up there and get my homework done before dinner, huh?"

He zoomed up to his room before his father could reply.

··· Chapter 5 ···
NOT READY

At practice the next afternoon, Daniel was feeling nervous. He knew Coach Turnbull might talk to him about starting at the next game. He also knew he had embarrassed himself in the last game when he tried to drive to the basket.

The team was in their practice uniforms, sitting on the bleachers. Coach T was standing on the court looking at his clipboard.

"All right, guys," Coach T said. "Some bad news: Dwayne Illy will not be in school for a week starting this Thursday. That means he won't be around to play in the game against Killcreek on Thursday afternoon."

The team groaned. Daniel gulped.

"Aw, man, Dwayne!" Isaac Roth said. "You can't miss the game."

Dwayne shrugged. "It's not my choice, guys," he said. "What can I do? I asked if I could stay home, but my mom and dad said no way."

"Everyone settle down," Coach Turnbull said. "We have a second-string team because sometimes guys can't make the game. Luckily, we have a player to take Dwayne's place. Daniel Friedland will start at small forward."

A few guys groaned again. Daniel slouched on the bleachers.

"Daniel's foul shot has really improved this season," Coach Turnbull went on, ignoring the groans. "He's going to be a real asset from the line."

Daniel was glad to hear the coach say that, but he could still feel the eyes of his teammates on him. No one was happy Dwayne wouldn't be around for the Killcreek game.

And to be honest, Daniel thought, *I'm not so happy about it either.*

After about a half hour of practice, Coach Turnbull gave a couple of sharp blows on his whistle. "Dwayne," he called out. "Take ten minutes. Do some laps or something."

"Seriously, Coach T?" Dwayne said. He spun the basketball on one finger. "I'm in the middle of drills."

"I see that," the coach replied. "And I want Daniel to take over at small forward in the drills for a little while."

Daniel looked up from the other end of the gym. He and the second-string players had been playing some half court.

"You got it, Coach," Dwayne said. He tossed the ball to Isaac and started a lap.

Daniel looked over at the other second-stringers. Sam shrugged at him. "Looks like you've been promoted," Sam said. "For now."

Daniel sighed and walked down the court toward Isaac and the other starters.

"Hi," Daniel said.

The four boys looked at him, then at each other. "Let's do this," Isaac said.

Isaac dribbled up to the top of the key and raised his right hand, showing two fingers.

Daniel knew what he was supposed to do. It was the same play Daniel had seen Isaac and Dwayne do in lots of games during the season.

Isaac would fake a shot, Dwayne would cut across the key, and Isaac would move up the left side as he passed the ball to Dwayne. Then Dwayne was supposed to drive hard to the hoop.

Daniel could do what he'd seen Dwayne do. "I can do this," Daniel muttered to himself.

Daniel looked at Isaac. Isaac pumped once, then cut to his left. Daniel quickly ran across the key just as Isaac's pass came through.

Daniel caught the pass, spun, and drove to the hoop.

On his last dribble before the shot, though, the ball hit his forward foot and flew out of bounds.

Coach Turnbull blew his whistle.

"You feeling all right, Daniel?" the coach called out.

"I'm fine," Daniel replied. He looked at Isaac. "Let's take it from the top. Sorry."

Isaac shook his head as the assistant coach tossed the ball back in. Then he held up two fingers again to start the play.

Daniel cut across the key and caught the pass just fine. He looked down the lane, and drove to the hoop. He went up for the layup. . . .

Brick!

The ball thudded hard into the side of the hoop and ricocheted into the bleachers. Coach Turnbull's whistle was piercing this time.

"Daniel," he called out. "Come over here."

Daniel took a deep breath and jogged over to the coach.

"I know, I know," Daniel said as he stepped up to the coach. "I must just be a little nervous."

Coach Turnbull put a hand on Daniel's shoulder. "Scott Dean has been working hard on his ball handling," the coach said. Scott was a second-string guard.

"Yeah," Daniel said, "he's gotten pretty good."

"Scott might have a little less trouble with those drives that are breaking up your game this afternoon," Coach T went on.

"Wait a minute," Daniel said. "What are you saying?"

The coach sighed. "Your foul shot has really improved. Everyone's noticed," he said. "But maybe you're not quite ready to start at small forward after all."

··· Chapter 6 ···
GIVE UP

"I don't know what to do," Daniel said. He was walking home again, but this time his friend Jimmy Kim was walking with him. Jimmy was the sports writer for the school newspaper.

"This might be my only chance to start, since Dwayne is out of town," Daniel said. "But let's face it. I'm not good enough. Maybe it would be easier to just let Scott take my place."

Jimmy shrugged. "I suppose it would be easier," he said.

"You think I should just give up?" Daniel asked, a little surprised.

"I didn't say that," Jimmy said. "I just agreed it would be easier to give up."

"Oh, I see," Daniel said with a roll of his eyes. "You're being wise, huh?"

Jimmy laughed. "It's the only way I know how to be," he said. "Look, my point is this. From the line you're as good as Dwayne Illy, right?"

"I don't know. Maybe," Daniel said.

"I've seen his stats," Jimmy said, "and yours. Plus I've seen you at the park, just shooting foul shot after foul shot. You're as good, if not better."

"Okay," Daniel said.

"Now, your game from the floor," Jimmy went on, "that's another story."

"You're telling me," Daniel said. "I'm a mess."

"You're not that bad," Jimmy said. "I get that practice didn't go so well, but I know you don't normally dribble off your own foot. You're better than that. It sounds like today was way worse than normal."

"Man, it was awful," Daniel said, remembering how embarrassed he'd been at practice.

"You do throw a heck of a brick now and then, though," Jimmy added.

"Hey!" Daniel protested.

"So, you've got four days," Jimmy went on. "It's not ideal, but you can practice, and get your drive down."

"You want me to just stroll up to Coach T and say, 'Hey, Coach. I have to practice my game from the floor, so let's just focus on me between now and game day'?" Daniel said.

The two boys reached the corner of Main and Eighth Street. Jimmy's family lived to the left, and Daniel's to the right. "Look, I gotta head home," Jimmy said. "But you worked on your foul shot all season without help from the coach or the practices. Why can't you do the same with your drives? Anyway, I'll see you."

Daniel stood on the corner as Jimmy walked away. "He's right," Daniel muttered to himself. "I've done it before. I can do it again."

He turned to his right and started toward home. To his surprise, a group of old men were sitting on a nearby bench, watching him.

"Also," he added quickly, "I really have to stop talking to myself."

··· Chapter 7 ···

The next morning, Daniel was up early, as always. He headed to the park to practice. But that morning, instead of shooting foul shot after foul shot, Daniel practiced his layups.

He stood at the top of the key, then dribbled up one side of the lane. He tried not to think about bouncing the ball off his foot, or throwing up a brick. He tried to just focus on making the shots.

As he reached the bottom of the key, he jumped, raised the ball, and gently released it. It hit the backboard, circled the rim, and fell out.

"Well," Daniel said, grabbing the rebound, "better than last time, at least."

For an hour, Daniel took layup after layup, sometimes from the left and sometimes from the right. By the end of his practice session, he had made a few shots. Still, it wasn't quite what he needed. He needed to make all the shots.

* * *

When Daniel got to school later that morning, he found PJ Harris and Isaac Roth hanging out by their lockers.

"Hi, PJ. Hey, Isaac," he said.

The two starters looked at him for a moment.

"What's up, Daniel?" Isaac said.

"You guys know I, um, might be starting in the next game, right?" Daniel asked.

Isaac and PJ looked at each other, then nodded.

"Listen, I know I'm not the best ball handler on the team," Daniel went on.

Isaac laughed. "Not even close," he said. PJ chuckled.

Daniel pretended not to hear that. "My foul shot is good," he said. "Jimmy Kim thinks I might have the best shot from the line on the team."

Isaac seemed impressed. But he said, "So what's your point?"

"I need your help, both of you," Daniel said. "PJ, you can block anything, practically, since you're the tallest guy on the team."

"Tallest in the league," PJ corrected him.

"Okay," Daniel said, turning to Isaac. "And you're the best defender on the team, right?"

"Most steals in the league since the 1980s," Isaac said, smiling.

"Right," Daniel said. "But PJ, you also get called for shooting fouls, and Isaac, you get called for reaching in."

"You better have a point," PJ said, frowning down at Daniel.

"I want to practice driving on you two," Daniel said quickly, "so I can play well in the game, and get to the foul line to score."

Isaac and PJ looked at Daniel for a long time. A bell rang, letting them know homeroom would be starting in two minutes.

"So?" Daniel asked nervously. "Will you help?"

"The game is in three days," Isaac replied. "How are we going to have time to practice, just the three of us?"

"I'm at the park courts every day at six," Daniel replied.

"Man, I can't go practice at six," PJ said. "I have dinner with my dad, and then do my homework."

"No, six in the morning," Daniel explained.

Isaac and PJ just about fell over. "In the morning?" Isaac said. "That's insane!"

"It's how I got my foul shot so good," Daniel said. "Look, we better get to homeroom. Think about it. And then be at the court at six tomorrow morning."

With that, Daniel jogged down the hall and got to class just in time.

··· Chapter 8 ···
TWO-ON-ONE

The next morning, the grass was wet, and a mist hung over the court. Daniel jogged up with his hood on and his coat zipped up to his neck.

He was almost surprised to see two people on the court already. One of them was very, very tall.

"Hey," Isaac called to him. "We were afraid you weren't showing up."

"It would have been the meanest prank ever," PJ added. "There would have been revenge."

Daniel laughed. "Well, I made it, so please don't hurt me," he said.

He went right to the foul line, raised his ball, and sank an easy swish.

"Nice shot," PJ said.

Isaac grabbed the rebound and passed it to Daniel. "Courtesy," he said.

Daniel dribbled once, then shot. Another swish.

This time PJ grabbed the rebound. "You ever miss?" he asked. He passed the ball back to Daniel.

Daniel spun the ball between his palms. "Sure," he said. "Watch this."

He drove up the left side of the lane and tried for the layup. The ball hit the center of the backboard and fell past the other side of the rim.

"See?" Daniel said. He jogged after the ball as it rolled off the court.

"And that's why we're here," Isaac said. "Right?"

"Exactly," Daniel replied. "If I can score from the floor, there's a chance the defense will foul me. And we know I can score from the line."

"Then what are we waiting for?" Isaac said. "Let's play a little two-on-one."

··· **Chapter 9** ···

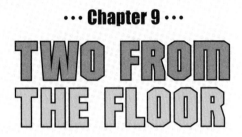

TWO FROM THE FLOOR

Daniel met with PJ and Isaac on the courts for the next two mornings. By the time team practice came around the day before the game, Daniel was feeling pretty good about his layups.

The team sat on the bleachers and Coach Turnbull stood before them. "To get ready for game day, and to help me choose a starting small forward," he said, "we're going to play some five-on-five today."

Coach T looked at his clipboard. "Now, as you probably noticed, Dwayne is off to his family reunion already," the coach went on, "so small forward on the red team will be Daniel."

"The four starters, split between red and blue," Coach T said, "and the rest of the second-string, fill in the gaps. Let's get started."

PJ and Isaac both ended up on Daniel's team. They both gave him a high five after they'd all pulled on their red scrimmage jerseys.

"You feel ready?" Isaac asked.

Daniel nodded. "Definitely," he said. "Those guys don't know what they're in for."

Daniel was right.

The coach blew his whistle to start play. The red team got possession first and PJ passed to Isaac.

Isaac held the ball at the top of the key, looking for Daniel. Isaac held up two fingers, calling the play.

Daniel cut across the key and caught Isaac's pass. He spun to his left, then to his right. Then he drove to the hoop.

Hank Jones, the second-string center, barely tried to stop the drive. Like the rest of the team, he thought Daniel was no good from the floor. But Daniel surprised everyone.

With one long step, Daniel jumped. He loosely let the ball glide off his hand. It hit the backboard gently and fell in for two points.

"Nice one, Daniel," PJ called.

Isaac held up his palm for a high five. "Nice layup," he said.

Daniel slapped his hand. "Now they know I can shoot," he said.

Isaac nodded. "So now we go with plan B," he said.

··· Chapter 10 ···

NEW STARTER

On the blue team's first possession, Scott proved what a great ball handler he was. He took a pass outside the key, then drove to the hoop. He fooled three defenders and went for a layup. PJ was right in his face, though.

Coach T blew his whistle. "Foul," he called. "Watch the arm, PJ."

So Scott went to the line.

Daniel already knew Scott's ball handling was great, but he hadn't seen him shoot too many foul shots before. Scott stood at the line, took a deep breath, and shot. The ball hit the backboard too low. It launched off the back of the rim, right back to Scott.

"One more, one more," the coach said. "Make it a good one."

The players on the sides of the lane got ready to go for the rebound. PJ bounced lightly on his toes. Scott raised the ball for his second shot and let it go.

PJ jumped and got the rebound. Daniel turned and headed up the court. PJ's pass was perfect. Daniel took it right to the hoop, but Hank Jones was right next to him. The coach's whistle sounded again.

"Foul, Hank," Coach T said. "Take the line, Daniel."

"This is our game now," Isaac said, smiling. Scott gave him a nasty look.

Coach T handed Daniel the ball. Daniel spun it between his palms and faced the basket. He raised the ball, exhaled, and shot.

Swish!

"Nice shot," Isaac said, clapping. "Nice shot."

"One more," the coach said. PJ tossed the rebound to the coach, who handed the ball to Daniel.

Daniel held the ball up, lined up the shot, and let it go. The ball hit the backboard and fell in.

"That's two more points," Coach Turnbull said. "Blue ball."

* * *

Daniel went on to score twenty points in the scrimmage. The red team beat the blue team easily. At the end of practice, Daniel, Isaac, and PJ were celebrating.

"Daniel, come talk to me for a minute," Coach Turnbull said.

"What's up, Coach T?" Daniel said. He took a seat on the bench and faced his coach.

"So, Daniel," Coach Turnbull said, "you sure have improved a lot, especially on those layups."

"Thanks," Daniel said. "But I don't deserve all the credit. Isaac and PJ practiced with me a lot the last few days."

The coach looked surprised. "They did?" he asked. "When?"

"They met me at the public courts before school," Daniel said. "I'm always down there, usually to practice free throws."

"I'm really impressed with your attitude, Daniel," the coach said. "That makes me even more sure of this decision. I have no problem with starting you in the game tomorrow. I'm sure you'll do well."

"Thanks, Coach T," Daniel replied.

"Dwayne is going to move up to the high school team next year," the coach said. "That means I'll be looking for a new starting forward!"

Daniel's mouth fell open. "Really?" he asked.

The coach nodded. "Yes," he said. "So how would you like to be our new small forward?"

Daniel jumped to his feet and smiled. "That would be great!" he said. "I'll keep practicing too, every morning."

The coach laughed. "I believe it," he said. "Now go get showered and rest up for tomorrow. Maybe take tomorrow morning off, huh?"

Daniel headed to the locker room and opened his locker. His uniform was there, still nearly as clean as the day he got it. "I'll have to bring that home after tomorrow's game," he said to himself. "I'll finally break a sweat on game day."

BY JAKE MADDOX

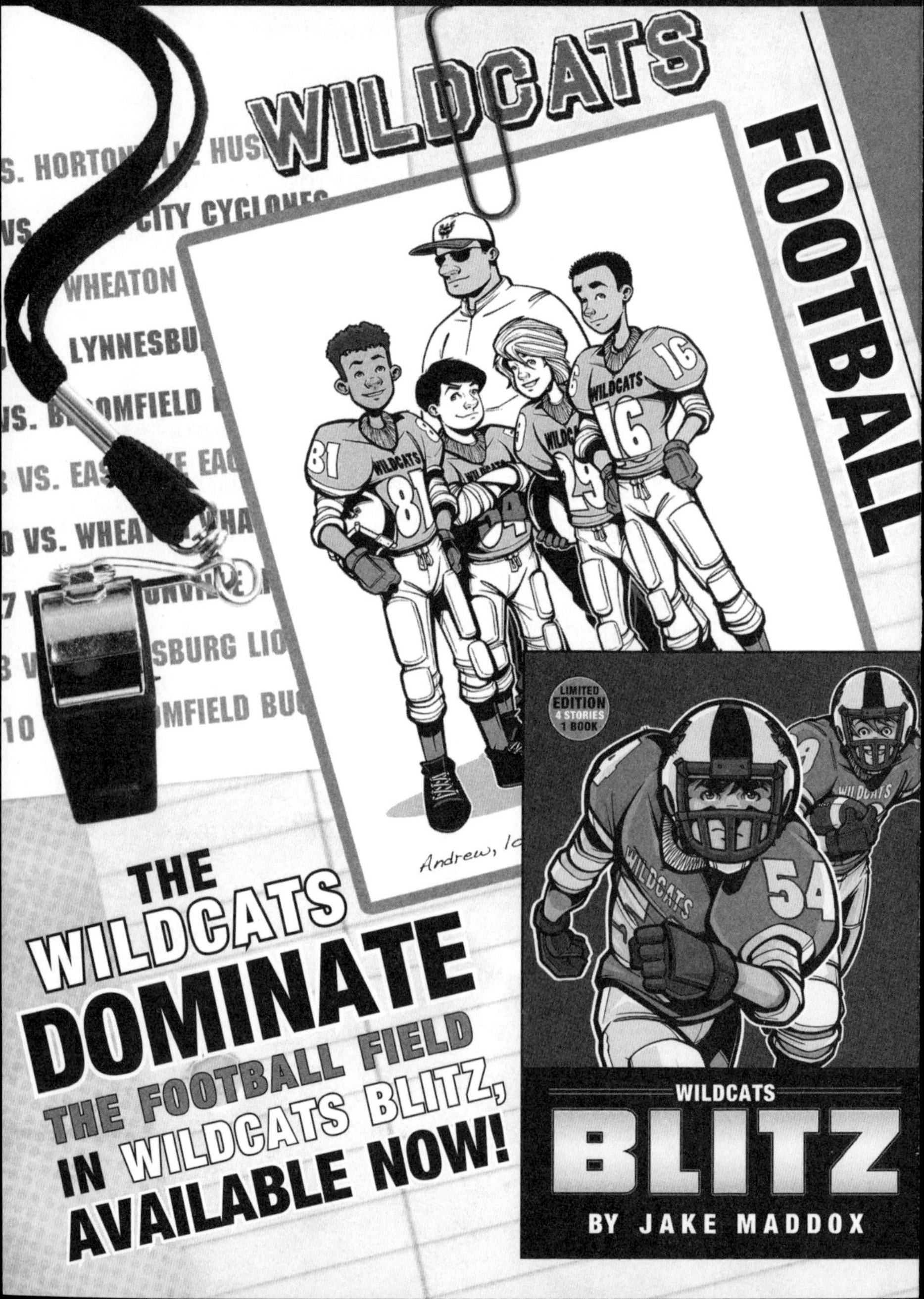